They Came From Sweden

Sod-House Winter

*. . . a single sheet of newspaper.   He spread it
out for Gustaf to see.   (See Chapter Six.)*

They Came From Sweden

Sod-House Winter

CLARA INGRAM JUDSON

Illustrated by EDWARD C. CASWELL

CHICAGO NEW YORK

Books by Clara Ingram Judson

Abraham Lincoln, Friend of the People
Admiral Christopher Columbus
Andrew Carnegie
Andrew Jackson, Frontier Statesman
Benjamin Franklin
Bruce Carries the Flag
George Washington, Leader of the People
The Lost Violin
Michael's Victory
The Mighty Soo
Mr. Justice Holmes
Petar's Treasure
Pierre's Lucky Pouch
Reaper Man, The Story of Cyrus Hall McCormick
St. Lawrence Seaway
Sod-House Winter
Theodore Roosevelt, Fighting Patriot
Thomas Jefferson, Champion of the People
Yankee Clippers, The Story of Donald McKay

For Younger Readers

Abraham Lincoln
Christopher Columbus
George Washington

Library of Congress Catalog Card Number: 57-8276

SIXTH PRINTING
Follett Publishing Company
1010 West Washington Boulevard
Chicago, Illinois 60607

T/L 8170

To
ALICE ANNE
ana
JIMMIE

CONTENTS

CONTENTS

They Came From Sweden

Sod-House Winter

THE JOURNEY FROM SWEDEN

Chapter One

G<small>USTAF</small> L<small>ARSSON</small> leaped up the uncarpeted stairway two
steps at a time and burst into the small bedroom.

'Elna! Hans! Wake up! Father says we are to have
breakfast! A good, *big* breakfast. How fine it smells!'

1

Elna stirred and curled herself into a tighter little roll. That way, she had learned, she didn't feel the aching hollow from hunger.

Gustaf laughed and shook her shoulder.

'Sleepyhead! Hear me! We're not on the old boat; this is the inn at Milwaukee. Father says, "Come to breakfast." '

'Breakfast? Real breakfast, Gus?' Elna and Hans sat up like Jack-in-the-box figures and stared hopefully at their older brother. He looked tall in the morning light; tall and very cheerful. His blond hair was neatly combed. His short blue coat was still grimy and limp from weeks of hard wear, but his thin face was clean and happy.

'Real breakfast,' he assured them. 'Can't you smell it?'

Elna and Hans sniffed. There *was* a good smell, for a fact. Surely that was pork cooking.

Elna reached under the bed and pulled forward two pairs of wooden shoes, dragging with them rolls of gray dust.

'Ugh! Mother will not like that!' She brushed off the dust and slipped her bare feet into her shoes. 'Here, Hans, put yours on.'

'Better hurry,' Gustaf reminded her. 'You're to tidy yourselves at the pump in the back yard. Father's been walking in the town and he has plans to tell us. We must not keep him waiting.'

Hans and Elna scrambled down the stairs after their big brother; followed him out the back door. A wooden pump surrounded by mud stood in a bare, untidy back yard.

'I'll pump,' said Gustaf. 'Stand on that board, now,

2

and wash.' Elna rubbed her hands in the water and dashed a few drops on her face.

'Don't waste it, Gus. That's enough.'

'Oh, take all you want, there's plenty! See how fast I can pump?' He sent the handle up and down briskly and great spurts of water dashed from the spout. 'Wash again! It's fun! Father says it's only on the boat that water is scarce. Now that we are come ashore, there's plenty. Isn't that a silly joke?'

Elna and Hans thrust hands and faces under the cool water, shook off all they could, and smoothed their hair and clothes. Elna's dark red homespun dress and gray apron were soiled and travel-stained, but she tidily pulled the apron into place.

They followed Gustaf into the brick inn, down the hall through a door on the right, and into a square dining-room where people sat at three tables, eating. Their father and uncle were talking busily. Mrs. Larsson motioned the children to chairs pulled up ready before bowls of steaming porridge.

'Have plenty of sugar, Elna,' her father turned to say. 'It costs just the same. And cream. You'll think it a little thin, but it's good. There's corn bread and pork to come.' He finished drinking a great cup of coffee and smiled at them, alert and pleased. Safe they were, and done with the boat. They were sick of boats. June was the time to be on land.

It was the first day of March when Carl Larsson and his family left Sweden for the long journey to America, though the unsettling stir of planning began long before that. Harvest had been poor the summer before and letters from Cousin Axel Larsson, settled in Chicago, sounded wonderful. Land was cheap, he wrote. Even a poor man could own a farm. And one could get an education. A poor farmer boy had a chance to be some-one in the world. Food was cheap, too, and work well paid. It read like a fairy tale to a poor tenant farmer in Sweden that fall of 1855, for land there was barren and stony and a man could not hope to buy any. Laws then were not as favorable for humble folk as later. His chil-dren could learn to read and figure but they would al-ways be poor peasants, Carl Larsson knew. What was the use of being strong and willing if you could not better yourself or your children?

All that winter as they sat hugging the stove, evenings, Carl and his pretty wife, Anna Marie, talked about America. Carl's parents were dead, his older brother settled miles away; he had only his seventeen-year-old brother, Ernst, who could go with them. Anna Marie's parents were not so old — maybe some day they and her younger sister Greta could come to America, too, when Carl and Anna Marie had made a home.

In February of 1856 the Larssons sold their cow and pigs, the flock of chickens and geese, and their few pieces of furniture. They took down the spinning wheel and loom and packed the parts between folds of bedding. The small churn was filled with garden seeds, each vari-ety tied in a separate little bundle and marked. The washing paddle, the copper kettle, the coffee mill, the axe, two knives, and other small possessions were packed with woollen shawls, clothes, and lengths of homespun cloth and tied into bundles. A great one, the heaviest, was for the father to carry. Ernst and the mother had bundles only a little less heavy. Gustaf, being twelve and strong for his age, carried his full share. Elna, being but eight, had a smaller one, and Hans carried the bread sack, for he was only five. When everything was ready, good-byes were said and they set out.

They walked to Göteborg and waited two weeks before Larson finally made a bargain with a sailing-master whose boat, the *Charles Tottie*, was taking a load of iron to New York. The captain judged the trip would take about eight weeks, and the twenty passengers he agreed at the last minute to carry would be clear profit, for he merely promised them deck and cabin room. They had to provide their own food and bedding. But storms came up, and it was eleven weeks before they landed, weary and hungry, in New York.

Carl Larsson wasn't afraid of the strange city. By paying close attention on the voyage he had learned to understand a few English words and he knew just what to do, for Cousin Axel had written: 'Go across the city as quickly as you can. Everything costs much money. Take the steamboat to Albany. There you can get the canal packet to Buffalo. Tell Anna Marie to buy food at the market two blocks from the steamboat landing in New York. You can get more in Albany, where food costs less.'

The ride on the packet was the best part of the whole journey. May sunshine made New York State green and fragrant. Wild apple trees bloomed; the children played on the canal bank now and then when the tow-team was late. Clothes were washed in a borrowed tub and dried on deck as the mules pulled the packet gently toward Buffalo.

But the lake trip was bad. Storms hit the creaking boat

before they left Lake Erie, and coming around the straits the captain feared they would all be drowned. He hugged the Wisconsin shore all the way down from Port Washington and finally, at late twilight, landed them unexpectedly in Milwaukee.

'Stay here or get yourselves to Chicago — take your choice. And no fares back!' he roared as someone started to ask a question. 'You're lucky not to be at the bottom of the lake. Wisconsin's a good place — what's the matter with it? There's a stage to Chicago and plenty of other boats. Take a steam train if you have the fare. I'm done.'

There was nothing for his passengers to do but gather up their bundles and get off. He was right. They were lucky to be alive and on land.

Elna had been so sleepy she'd hardly noticed when her father carried her up the stairs in the small two-story inn near the dock. As for Hans, he was sound asleep, worn out with excitement, long before Ernst dumped him on the bed and hurried back for the bundles Gustaf was guarding behind a pile of lumber by the dock.

This morning at sunup Larsson left to explore the city and see what he could find. His grin as he looked at the children now showed that he liked his discoveries.

'Such luck you never heard, Anna Marie,' he said between mouthfuls. 'I found Herr Lange himself, just back from a trip to Chicago. You remember Fru Bremer wrote about him in the letter the minister read to us? He knows we want to see Axel. But he says: "Why not settle here where the land is beautiful as it is in Sweden, with rivers and lakes and hills, not flat like a tabletop as Chicago? Get your farm and be settled," he says.

6

"Then go see your cousin." Settled. Sounds good!' He grinned at his family and took a hunk of hot corn bread from a platter the innkeeper's wife set before him.

'And so then?' The mother could hardly wait to hear more. Hungry as she was, she watched him eagerly. Eating could come later. The children spooned porridge and listened.

'Herr Lange has just the place for us. Out by Nashotah where Gustaf Ononius settled in '41. To think *we* should settle there!' Larsson was amazed at the turn of fate. 'You remember, Wife, his letters that we read in the paper?'

'Aye,' answered Mrs. Larsson. 'And my father heard him talk in the church when he came back to Sweden. Ononius said America was a fine place, Carl.'

'That it must be.' He paused to finish his second cup of coffee. 'We can get ten acres by Pine Lake. Pearman, who had it, moved to Chicago. There is a cabin. A garden plot was broken, though it has not been worked for three years.'

'We can rent it, Father?' Gustaf asked. 'Here, Hans, take all you want. Father says it costs no more.' He leaned across to spoon three great helpings of soft yellow sugar from the coarse earthen bowl to Hans's porridge. The innkeeper's wife grinned at Gustaf, then took the bowl to the kitchen for refilling. She knew boys liked sugar.

'Rent!' The father laughed gleefully. 'You shall see! Now I shall buy a spade and a grub-hoe at Lange's store. And a bucket. That's about all we can carry. Lange says we can buy a cow on the way. Pack the

7

bundles as tightly as you can, Wife. Twenty-five miles is a walk for you and the children after you've been cooped up on the boat like chickens going to market.' He pulled Elna's thick braids affectionately.

'Not for me,' Elna boasted proudly. 'I can run and carry a load, too. I could walk to Chicago!'

'I can walk as far as a girl can!' Hans cried. 'I can carry a load, too.'

'Good for you, children; we'll try you out this afternoon. Gus, your mother will be packing. Stay by and see if she needs anything. Don't let the children get lost. Ernst will go with me to carry the tools. Better have the bundles at the door in two hours, Wife. We've no money to stay here longer.' He pushed back his chair, straightened his blue coat proudly, and went across the hall and into the office to pay for lodging and breakfast. Carl Larsson always paid his way promptly. 'If you haven't the money in your pocket, don't buy,' he always said, and his neighbors in Sweden respected him.

'What will the new home be like, Mother?' Gustaf asked as he turned to finish his breakfast. 'Father says, "Like Sweden." We left Sweden.'

'He means pretty country, Son; didn't you hear him speak of lakes and hills? Sweden is pretty to look at, but the land is poor for making a living. America is rich but pretty, too. Finish your corn bread, Hans. Here's some honey, Elna. It tastes good.'

'Shall we get there tonight, Mother?'

'Twenty-five miles in one day, Elna? You must be thinking about the teacher's Hans Christian Andersen fairy-story book! We'll be lucky to make it there in *two* days with all our bundles and a new way to find.'

'Is there another inn?' Hans licked off the sugary spoon. He liked this inn.

'Maybe we'll sleep out,' suggested Elna.

'Maybe we'll find some Indians,' said Gustaf. 'That would be something to write in a letter to send home. Indians.'

'Indians are people. We are people.' His mother's voice was almost stern. 'They are copper-skin and I hope you shall see them. But don't believe all the wild tales you heard on the boat, Son. . . . Finish your breakfast, children. See, the others are leaving.'

People from the other tables got up and strolled out, talking briskly in English and German. The Larssons, of course, spoke only Swedish, though they were trying to learn English words as fast as they could. English would be useful in the new land.

'You may walk to the corner and look about,' the mother said. 'But don't go far. Your father will come and we must be ready.'

Chapter Two

THE sun was high in the sky when the children saw their father striding down the narrow street toward the inn. Even at a distance, they saw his pleased look.

'We set out at once!' he said. 'Is your mother ready?'

'She has repacked all the bundles to carry better, Father,' Gustaf answered. 'Now she is in the kitchen bargaining for food to take with us.'

'Good. Run tell her I am here.'

The mother met him in the hall.

'We go,' he said. Nothing else. And she asked no questions.

'The bundles are ready, in the hall. Gus, you fetch Hans.'

As Gustaf went through the kitchen, the innkeeper's wife dropped a small parcel into his coat-pocket. She put her fingers on her lips to show it was a secret, for him.

'Thank you! Thank you!' he said in Swedish, and smiled at her, delighted with a surprise.

'For your porridge,' she told him in German, and pointed to a porridge bowl to tell her meaning.

In ten minutes they were off, Larsson ahead, a great load swung over his left shoulder, the mother next; Ernst, Gustaf, Elna, each carried as much as possible. The bread sack Hans carried was full. Loads were heavier than when they left home. New tools, a jug of molasses (sugar was too costly), coffee, and other supplies added weight.

Away from the dock, streets were wider, houses newer, mostly made of yellowish brick, cheerful and elegant. Trees made pleasant shade. People seemed prosperous.

Elna ran to catch up with her father and mother.

'It is nice here. Is it like Stockholm?'

'No, Stockholm is different again.' The mother tried to recall the one visit she had made in Stockholm as a little girl. 'I like this better. This is America.'

The sun slanted lower. Houses were fewer. The open country spread before them.

'I might have eaten more for breakfast if I had tried,' Gustaf said regretfully. 'There was plenty.' He fingered the parcel in his pocket anxiously. Was it food? Likely as not: it came from the kitchen. Should he eat it now? The innkeeper's wife had motioned to a porridge bowl; something to eat with porridge, he thought she meant;

11

or in a bowl. He liked having a secret. He looked at Elna and quickly took his hand from his pocket, lest she see.

'You would need to put it in your jacket, then,' giggled Elna. 'You told me there was no more room in your stomach. And maybe there is a law about taking away food you cannot eat.'

'The light will last for hours yet,' the father decided suddenly. 'We rest, now, and eat.'

They dropped bundles by the side of the narrow road. How good it felt to be free of burdens! Gustaf stretched his muscles and turned three skillful cartwheels to take away the ache. Elna sat on the grass by Hans. The mother untied the bread sack. She had a fine surprise for them, corn bread and cold fish fried with a taste of salt pork. Gustaf fingered his secret but decided to wait. The food looked good. He was very hungry.

'It is a good thing for us that our countryman lives in Milwaukee and that I found him,' Larsson said when he had finished eating. 'He told me much I needed to know. He took me to the land agent and I have the papers now. Ten acres of good land. And a cabin with a chimney and a good fireplace.'

'A fireplace, Father?' exclaimed Gustaf. 'You did not expect that!'

'Aye, Son, we are lucky. He says the cabin is a small one, loosely built — but the chimney draws well. Pearman built it eight years ago.'

'We work the land for him?' The mother had wondered.

'We work the land for the new owner, *me*.' Carl Larsson stood up and bowed to his family. Their amazed

12

stares made the surprise even better than he had planned.

'Owner? You? Have you bought it already?' His wife couldn't believe, and as for the children, their eyes were big with amazement.

'I paid the agent. Forty dollars. The papers are in my pocket now.'

'And you didn't tell us all this time!' cried the mother.

'It is better to hear now, while we rest. A man does not buy land and keep his family in an inn *two* nights!' He chuckled at the thought of such folly.

The mother rose quickly and began repacking the bread sack.

'Come! Why do we idle here? Gus, you have eaten enough already! Hans, the sack is lighter now, you can walk fast. If we keep going till dark, maybe we can get there by tomorrow night.'

'Easy enough three months ago, Wife,' Larsson said kindly as he swung his bundle up. 'But we are soft, now. Twenty-five miles is a long walk for the children.'

'We shall begin to get hard now,' replied his wife. 'We have work to do.'

That night they slept on the grass by hazelnut bushes; before sunup they were on the way again. The country was beautiful, green and fresh; wild flowers bloomed, birds sang. They passed half a dozen cabins during the morning — German settlers. The coach bound for Watertown and Madison drove by, lurching through ruts in the road.

'First thing when we get there, we shall have a bath,' planned the mother.

'Not so,' objected the father. 'You shall bake us some good food.'

13

'Baths first, though. I wish we had some milk. A cow would be useful, Carl.'

'Lange told me of a man out here,' Larsson remembered. 'Pederssen, a Norwegian. We should come to his place this afternoon. Lange says he will sell us flour and a cow.'

'You mean we buy us a cow today?' exclaimed the mother.

'How else shall we get one? That is the way they do business in America. Quick! Make up your mind! Buy! It's a good way — if you have the money.'

The mother was thoughtful. A dollar and a half for lodging and breakfast. Forty dollars for the land. A cow to buy, food until harvest, seed. Would there be money enough? She pondered as she followed the others, west.

'Walk with me, Hans,' said his father. He noticed the little boy was lagging. 'See that squirrel up in the oak? He knows which tree has the acorns. Now we shall sing. Music makes the load light. Where's your harmonica, Gus?'

Gustaf shifted his load, pulled his harmonica from his inside pocket and thrust it between his lips. They began with the old favorite, 'The Herdsman's Song,' and sang right through a dozen. The road was a mere trail now, with here and there a creek to cross, and once a lake glimpsed in the distance.

'I see a house!' cried Gustaf.

'I hear a bell,' said Elna. 'Maybe someone has a cow.'

On ahead was a small house, neatly built of sawed lumber. It had a mill-made door and two windows; a

14

roof high enough for a loft. Behind it were a lean-to and a snug log barn.

The first to notice the approaching travelers was a girl about Elna's age. She fetched her mother, and by the time the Larssons were close by, five people had gathered to greet them, calling welcome in Norwegian. Any Scandinavian language would have sounded like music after the weeks and weeks of hearing only English and German!

'You shall stay the night,' Mrs. Pederssen planned hospitably. 'My Nels and Anton shall sleep on the floor and you shall have the loft to yourselves.'

'But we are travel-stained,' Mrs. Larsson objected, suddenly ashamed.

'Fret not,' laughed Mrs. Pederssen. 'We were all that way when we first came. Bundles and dirt! Five years ago I thought we never, never would get ourselves clean again!'

'There is plenty to eat and drink, what with the cow I cannot sell and the greens I dug this morning.' She bustled about happily, proud to have people from the old country see how well the Pederssens had done for themselves.

'Lange, in Milwaukee, told me I might buy a cow on the way,' began Larsson.

'Our Blossom, I'll be bound. A better cow you'll not find in all of Wisconsin. But with all the milk from Victoria, and Snuggle coming fresh soon, we want to sell her.'

'I'll buy if I can strike a bargain,' said Larsson.

'Good cows are eight dollars around here and no bargain to be haggling over. My man will be coming home soon. You talk to him. But come now and eat; you are all weary. I shall never forget how long the way seemed when we walked out from Milwaukee the first time.' She talked along cheerfully as they washed and ate.

Supper was delicious; wheat bread with fresh butter such as they hadn't eaten since they left home; greens and tasty salt pork. Sweet bread and wild plum jam was for the finish, with coffee for the grownups and milk for the children. Finally Mrs. Larsson made motions to Gustaf to take no more. But Mrs. Pederssen generously set another basket of bread before her own Nels and Anton and urged them all to eat all they wanted.

After supper the children played by the plum tree. Hans went to sleep under its shelter and the others tossed jackstones in the twilight until mothers called them to bed. Grownups talked far into the night.

The next morning was sunny again, and after a good breakfast the Larssons started west. The cow they drove with them was sturdy and sleek, larger than a Swedish cow, and they eyed her admiringly. Mrs. Pederssen slipped rye cakes and cheese into the bread sack.

'Keep right along the road for about three miles,' Pederssen directed them, 'till you come to a low hill with four trees across the crest. Walk along the south edge of a small lake there till you come to a larger one. That's Pine Lake. Leave the road there; it goes on to the Norwegian settlement two miles west. From the high ground not a hundred yards north, you'll see a cabin and the marks Lange's cousin Pearman set. That's your place.'

'*Your place!*' The words had a wonderful sound! The Larssons would never be discouraged or poor again!

'*Your place!*' They thanked the kind Pederssens and started walking.

The children wished to run all the way. Parents, too, could hardly wait now that the long journey was nearly ended. But they should not tire Blossom. The milk and butter they expected her to provide was more important than an early sight of the new home. She poked along good-humoredly, nibbling a tuft of green here, a tender bunch of leaves there. Gustaf and Elna took turns holding the rope and leading her.

The sun was halfway toward noon when they came to the hill with four trees. They walked around the south edge of the lake, up a rise. There, to the west, a large lake sparkled blue in the June sunshine — Pine Lake.

'I see our cabin!' shouted Gustaf.

'I see it too,' cried Elna.

'Oh, Mother!' cried weary Hans, 'we're here!'

Chapter Three

GRASS and rushes grew thick and green by the water's edge. On the slope near the lake was a small log cabin. Panes of glass in one little window on the south side reflected sunshine; likely the door faced the water. Left of the cabin was a shed, barely large enough to shelter a cow and a couple of pigs. To the east, broken ground showed where a garden and a plowed field had been.

Without a word the children walked straight to the cabin. The door sagged on bent hinges; a west window had several broken panes. The small room was dirty and disorderly but they saw a fireplace of field stone, a well-built chimney, a one-legged bed, its rope springs frayed

18

and worn. Two shelves were pegged into the south wall; wood cluttered the hearth. The father and mother peered over the heads of the children and for a long moment no one spoke. Then the mother began planning.

'Gus, take your knife and get me short branches — stout ones, mind you. I'll be needing a broom. Ernst, bring the bundles near but don't set *one* inside this cabin till I get it cleaned. Hans, gather us wood; you'll find plenty of small stuff around. Elna, unpack the kettle and bring up water ready for when we have a fire. And fetch the soap, Daughter; that bed needs scrubbing. Aren't we lucky to have a house to work in!'

Carl Larsson watered Blossom at the lake and tied her securely near the shed. Then he hurried off to inspect the garden plot. By some lucky chance there might be some self-sowed stuff from Pearman's time.

Gustaf and Ernst whistled gaily, Elna and the mother hummed snatches of song as their hands worked.

In half an hour the broom was made, short branches tied firmly with homespun twine. Elna brushed the hearth and scrubbed it with sand. Ernst repaired the crane; Elna brought the kettle; Hans gathered wood and Gustaf fetched a great backlog. Soon the kettle boiled merrily.

'What shall I do now, Mother?' asked Hans.

'Get us leaves, Son, piles of leaves for towels. Later we shall scrub ourselves.' And by the time Hans had gathered three piles the others had the cabin tidy, the shelves washed, the windows shining. Gustaf had repaired the hinge on the door.

'When do we eat, Mother?' he asked, as he laid the hammer aside. 'The sun says afternoon.'

'There's no time yet for a meal, Gus,' Mrs. Larsson said firmly, 'but if you'll all wash you may have the snack Mrs. Pederssen gave us. Call your father. Where shall we eat? Some day we shall have a table your father will make and we'll be very grand.'

'Let's sit here, on the grass in the shade,' said Elna. 'I'll get the bread sack, Mother, you sit down. My hands are washed.'

They stretched out on the grass and enjoyed the rye bread and cheese.

'What next?' asked Gustaf. 'I'd like to swim and bathe.'

'Three hours of work in the garden comes first,' said the father. 'Do you think you are gentlemen and can bathe in the middle of the day? Cleanliness is good, yes, but we must grow food and gather wood.'

'Pooh! I can get wood,' boasted Hans. 'There's plenty close by. They were careless!'

'Not careless, Hans,' corrected the father. 'Unknowing. Pearman wasn't a farmer. He does well in Chicago. He is learning to take a picture in a box, like magic, Pederssen says. They call the picture a photograph. He makes a good living.

'Come on, boys.' He got up from the grass. 'I found some self-sowed beans, Gus, you better weed them; beans in a month will taste fine. Ernst and I spade the garden.'

'But when the sun is so' — Mrs. Larsson pointed through the trees — 'you are all to stop work and bathe. Later it may be cool. And not another night shall the Larssons be unwashed. Hear me, Carl!'

Gustaf started toward the garden; Elna and the mother

unpacked bundles and spread bedding and clothing and lengths of hand-woven material on the grass. This sun would soon take away the musty smell from the boat.

'We're lucky, Elna,' the mother remarked. 'A house all ready for us! A fine day to unpack and settle.'

'It's an old house,' said Elna doubtfully. She had been remembering Cousin Axel's accounts of great houses in Chicago. 'And small.'

'Old!' scoffed the mother. 'Small! What do you expect for forty dollars? A palace, maybe, and a hundred acres?' She shook a quilt briskly and smiled at her daughter. 'Wait till your father makes us furniture and the cabin will seem nice. Lay the shirts there, a clean one for each. People work better when they are clean, Elna. This is a fine place.'

'May I wear my best petticoat this afternoon, Mother?' Elna shook out a pretty skirt of red- and yellow-striped material and admired it proudly.

'No-o-o, better save it. But your everyday petticoat is dirty, truly.' Mrs. Larsson sat back on her heels and squinted at the sun. 'It's early yet. And a fine day for drying. You and I shall wash the clothes and bathe.'

'Hans!' she called to the little boy as he carried wood back of the cabin, 'come! Take your clothes off and scrub in the lake. Time you are clean, we'll have your clothes washed and dried.' Gaily she grabbed the pile of soiled clothes she had sorted out and ran toward the lake. 'Bring me the washing paddle and the soap, Elna,' she called over her shoulder. 'We can scrub with sand, but the clothes need soap.'

Down by the lake, to the right, grew a small clump of bushes and out from there ran a narrow sandbar.

Hans stripped, tossed aside his clothes, and ran out into the warm water. Oh, how good it felt to his skin!

'Stay near the shore, Hans. Elna and I wash the clothes. We cannot watch out for you. Sit where it is shallow and scrub.' Hans sat down and rubbed sand on his neck, his arms and legs, while Elna eyed him longingly.

She helped her mother soap the clothes and pound them with the paddle. Then, standing on a log a few feet away, the mother rinsed them well and Elna spread them on the bushes to dry. Last, they washed the shifts they'd had on and then waded out to scrub themselves. Elna rubbed handfuls of sand over herself and then lay down luxuriously in the warm, shallow water.

'It's more fun than the baths at home, isn't it, Hans! How funny I say it! This is home, now!'

Soon the washed clothes were crisp and dry. Elna and the mother brushed their long blonde hair and dressed, putting on fresh white caps and clean gray aprons.

'Now the beds. And porridge for supper,' planned the mother. She gathered up the clean things and started toward the cabin. 'It will be tasty and hot even without a sweet. One can't have everything in one day, indeed.'

In an hour, the well-aired bedding was folded and piled in a corner, the rope lacing on the one-legged bed repaired, quilts spread. A gay shawl with long knotted fringe from Mrs. Larsson's dower chest was hung on the north wall. Its red and blue and yellow tones caught the west sun and gave the cabin a cheerful look. The copper kettle hung from the crane; in an iron pot on the hearth, porridge bubbled.

'Call them now,' commanded the mother. 'There will be another day for work.'

Elna ran back to the garden plot.

'Father! Ernst! Gus! You are to come!'

'What have you done to yourself, child?' cried the father. He dropped his spade, wiped the sweat from his eyes, and stared at his daughter. Her hair, still hanging loose from its brushing, was a golden mass that gleamed as he looked toward the sun. The red homespun petticoat that had been so long grimy was fresh and crisp, her blouse of dainty gray linen was becoming, her cheeks rosy, her blue eyes laughing. Even her wooden shoes were scoured clean, like new.

'You are all to come and bathe in the lake,' she said primly, suddenly shy before their admiring looks. 'And scrub well with sand. Your clean clothes are by the bank; put the soiled ones by the bush. We'll wash them in the morning. Come quickly, Mother says.'

'You don't need to call me twice.' Gustaf laughed gleefully. 'Soon I'll be clean as you, Sister.' He set his hoe by the shed and ran to the lake, pulling off clothes on the way.

'We should work an hour more,' complained the father, but he followed Gustaf.

'The water feels fine, Father. We can work to-morrow!'

'Swim me on your back, Father,' called Hans.

'I'm coming!' He laughed good-humoredly, and dashed into the water. For an hour they played and swam and scrubbed and sunned. Then the father dressed, and milked Blossom. Gustaf, reminded by his emptiness that it was suppertime, fetched a flat stone for the porridge pot, and the mother called that supper was ready.

They sat on the thick grass in front of the cabin. The late afternoon sun was pleasant, the feel of clean clothes on clean skin was comfortable, the thought of warm, well-cooked porridge made their mouths water.

'Bring the Book, Wife,' Carl Larsson said. 'We shall read and give thanks before we eat.'

'Let me get it, Father!' Gustaf jumped up quickly. 'I carried it in my bundle, you know.'

'Aye, and we shall need it more than tools, Son.'

Gustaf ran and opened his bundle. In the center, wrapped in hanks of homespun yarn, were three small brown books — the Psalm Book, the Catechism, the Bible, their covers worn with daily use. He handled them reverently as he gave them to his father.

Larsson laid the Catechism and Psalm Book aside and opened the Bible. It was a small book, not more than three inches high; its pages thin, the Swedish type tiny.

He opened to the fly leaf.

'Bring me my writing box, Elna. We should by rights have my father's great Bible, here. Some day my brother shall write in it for me, in Sweden.' Elna set the writing box by him and the children watched as he wrote, 'This day, June 16, 1856, came to our farm by Pine Lake, Wisconsin.' He blew on the writing to dry it, shut the writing box, and turned the pages to the 121st Psalm.

'I will lift up my eyes to the hills,' he read. Gustaf looked to the north, where the hills were rolling and green almost like in Sweden. But with a difference: this was their *own* land. They bowed their heads reverently for the prayer at the end of the psalm and then sang the evening hymn, 'While all the earth reposeth.' Then the mother fetched from the cabin the pot of steaming porridge.

Gustaf looked at it thoughtfully as she set it on the stone. The spell of the reading and the song made them quiet. Then he remembered!

'It's porridge!' He jumped up and ran into the cabin.

'Is the boy daft?' demanded the father. 'Now that we have a fire to cook it, what should we eat? "It's por-ridge," indeed!'

Inside the cabin Gustaf thrust his hand into the pocket of his blue coat and took out the parcel the innkeeper's wife had given him. Without delaying to open it, he hurried to the surprised group waiting outside, the par-cel held out in his hand.

'She gave it to me,' he said. 'The innkeeper's wife in Milwaukee gave it to me. It is a secret. "Porridge," she said. Now we have porridge.'

'The innkeeper's wife!' The mother could hardly be-lieve him. They stared as Gustaf unwrapped the cloth, undid the paper inside it — to show a mound of soft yellow sugar. Sugar such as the children had liked at the inn.

'She *gave* it to you!' exclaimed the father. 'What kindness!'

'Yes, for a surprise.' Gustaf was thrilled to be the bearer of such a treat. 'Our hands are clean. You may each take a pinch to put on the porridge.' The mother spooned the porridge and each in turn took a pinch of the precious yellow sugar. There was plenty for all. And it was very delicious.

'Work is good,' remarked Larsson when the porridge

pot was empty, 'but to rest is good, too.' He stretched out on the grass, refreshed by the hot supper. 'Play us a tune, Gus. Get out your harp, Ernst. Music ends the day well.'

Gustaf played a tune on his harmonica and Ernst strummed at his Jew's harp.

'Listen!' commanded Gustaf. He carefully played a few notes.

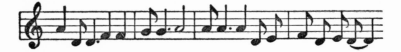

'I can play it!'

'That's the "Erie Canal Song," ' cried Elna. 'I know the chorus. I can sing it in English, Gus. The packet captain taught me.' She sang slowly, pronouncing each word with care;

> 'Low bridge, ev'rybody down!
> Low bridge, for we're going through a town.'

The mother clapped proudly. 'It's good to learn English, Elna.'

'There is another tune I learned on the packet,' remembered Gustaf. He played a few notes. 'I don't remember the English words. It's something about a star-spangled banner. It's a good song. Maybe we can learn it now that we are here.'

He looked around hopefully.

June twilight deepened across the lake. Frogs croaked faintly; fish made soft splashes; birds stirred, nesting. But there was no human sound. Gustaf had been too busy to think of it until now. Were there no neighbors?

THE NEW HOME

'Doesn't anyone live near here, Father? If we had neighbors they could teach us the song.' His father couldn't answer. The boy looked across the lake anxiously, little guessing that he himself would find the answer to that question — and change their lives.

HANS MAKES A DISCOVERY

Chapter Four

For the next two days the Larsson family worked their hardest. Father Larsson stepped off his land and made sure the markers were correct. Some immigrants had to take the word of strangers. Carl Larsson had learned the principles of surveying when as a youth he worked for the landlord at his father's home. Now he was thankful for that training. Then he and Ernst planned which land to plow, where to take wood for fuel; what to fence now and what to leave till autumn.

Meanwhile, Gustaf had set to work at once on the field Pearman had once plowed. Half-overturned stumps, stones, branches blown by wind, must all be removed so the crop could be planted at once. As soon as their planning was done, the father and Ernst helped with this field, too, and the work went quickly.

Then Gustaf chopped wood and stacked it back of the cabin. He cleaned the shed for Blossom and the pigs the father hoped to buy soon. Each morning he led Blossom out where the prairie grass was thick and green and left her tied to a tree where she could graze all day. In the evening, he brought her back and milked her. Blossom liked her new home and gave lots of rich milk.

Elna and her mother worked in the garden. Mrs. Larsson longed to bake. But porridge was nourishing, even without sugar, there was molasses once a day; and it was important to start the garden. The ground was soft and mellow, easy to work. The mother made shallow ditches and Elna crept after her, planting the precious seeds brought from Sweden. Not one should be wasted. Some day each seed would be a cabbage, a carrot, a beet, or a turnip. Elna's mouth watered at the thought and she patted the ground tenderly as she covered each seed.

The self-sowed beans looked fine now that they were worked and straightened.

'Here are some vines, Mother,' Elna discovered as she stood up before starting a new row.

'Maybe they are melons.' Mrs. Larsson came quickly to inspect. 'You remember Mr. Ononius said melons grew in America.'

'Yes, I remember. He said they were sweet and juicy. Do you suppose ——'

'Maybe.' Mrs. Larsson studied them hopefully. 'Be careful as you pull the weeds around them. They *might* be melons. Look out there, Son!' she shouted as Hans ran toward her. 'That's a melon, maybe. Don't step on the vine!'

'Could we eat it now, Mother?'

His mother sat back on her heels and laughed as she put her arm around him.

'Not today. Nor tomorrow. But *some* day. *Some* day there will be plenty of good food and you shall have all you want. Soon I shall find roots and maybe berries to help out till "some day" comes. We shall have enough.'

'Can't I help?'

'Yes, we need you. Find a small stout stick and stir the ground — so — ready for me to make the trench for the seeds. Soon Elna weeds the vines; maybe you can help her, too. But first bring me a drink. The sun is hot. You'll find water and the jug by the door.'

Hans ran down the slope toward the cabin. He might go north of the little house; or south by the shed, where there was a pretty pile of green vines. He chose the south way and, being in a hurry, he dashed right through the pile of green.

There was a shriek! And the small running boy disappeared.

Elna and her mother ran to him. Larsson in the woods, and Gustaf and Ernst, working in the field, all heard the cry and dashed toward the cabin.

Elna got there first. The pile of green had looked so pretty, she'd thought; almost like a fancy flower bed in the garden of a lord's estate. Now a great gap was torn through the center and at one side she spied a small, clinging hand.

'Hold on, Hans,' she commanded. 'Father comes! Hold on!' She knelt down and put her hand firmly over his wrist.

'It's a hole, Elna. I'm over a hole.' Hans's lips quivered but he didn't cry.

The mother bent down by Elna. 'Hold tight and don't

squirm, Son,' she told him quietly. 'Your father is near. A hole has a bottom, you know, and your father is strong. Here he is. And Gus, too. They will get you out.' That sounded comfortable.

But when the father arrived, running fast, the stir of his strong legs shook the heap of green and Hans was frightened again.

'Gus, go to the other side and lie flat on the ground before you reach out for Hans. Hold on, Elna! Hans, don't let go the vine there till Gus has your hand. Now! That's fine! They can hold you.

'Ernst, you and I shall pull the green away slowly. It's light stuff.' He began pulling, slowly, gently. They marveled at his quietness because usually the father was rough and fast in his work.

'It's a *well*, Hans! I'll declare it is! You are a discoverer and have to pay a little for your prize. Here's a strong stem. Hold that. There, now, hang on! Elna's still holding your wrist.' They watched as Hans slowly changed his right hand from a small useless stem to a strong, sturdy one; watched as the father pulled gently, so as not to loosen the hold or break a stem. Hans was pulled up, higher and higher. Hans was out of the hole and in his father's strong arms. The little boy sobbed with relief.

'Is it really a well, Father? Did I find something to help us?'

The father stretched himself out on the ground and peered down. Noontime sun threw light into the hole and, now that the brush was cleared away, reflected back from water. It was only a few feet below where Hans had hung.

31

'Yes, it is a well,' he finally replied. 'Pearman must have made it. Funny how a man could have a cabin and a well and leave for the city! Elna, get the kettle and we'll see what we can bring up.'

'Mind you leave the lid by the hearth,' warned the mother. 'We can't afford to lose anything.'

In a minute Elna was back with the uncovered kettle. Mr. Larsson unwound the rope he wore around his waist (a handy thing, a rope; often needed unexpectedly). The children watched as he tied it tightly to the kettle and slowly let it down.

Tipping the kettle sideways, he coaxed it over till the water rushed in, then hauled it up full to overflowing with clear, sparkling water.

'That looks good!' he said. 'We shall all drink.' He passed it to his wife first and then they each one drank in turn.

'Much better than the lake water,' approved the mother. 'No taste of weeds. We have wonderful luck in America. Water right by the house! Just wait till supper! I shall make fine coffee with this good water. You'll see!'

'We must lay some logs over the well,' planned the father. 'None of us shall fall in, for now we know it is here. But there's Blossom. A broken-legged cow wouldn't be such good luck, would it, Mother?'

'We could split logs and make it nice,' said Ernst. 'They wouldn't have to be so heavy.'

'But that will take time. We'll not stop to split them. It's more important to plant our crop at once. Whole logs will do for now.'

'If we only had a plow,' Ernst remarked.

32

'Wish us three,' said Larsson good-humoredly. 'A plow for you. A plow for Gus. A plow for me. How fast we'd get the crop in with three plows!'

'Ernst doesn't mean to joke, Father,' said Gustaf seriously. 'Maybe we could get a plow. The Pederssens said that there were Norwegians living at the other end of Pine Lake. Maybe we could borrow a plow.'

'Maybe.' The father studied the idea silently, then dismissed it. 'But we do not borrow. We have strong arms and a spade, haven't we?"

'But with a plow ——'

Larsson waved the words aside.

'The idea is good. Work goes well with a plow. But we have no money to spare. Still' — he rubbed his chin thoughtfully — 'it might be wise to find out how they do in America.' He wound the rope back about his waist. 'As soon as we get this well covered, you boys walk to the settlement and see what you find. That does no harm.'

'Wash before you go,' the mother reminded them. 'You must look nice. I'll get food ready. You can eat on the way.'

'We'll find out a lot, Father,' promised Gustaf as he ran toward the woods for logs. 'You shall see!'

Chapter Five

THE two boys set out in high spirits, pleased that they
were trusted with such an important errand.

'There ought to be good fish in this lake,' remarked

34

Ernst as they tramped along the shore. 'But it's shallow for pole fishing. If we had a boat we could get some. Fish would taste fine.' They stepped along briskly, eyes alert.

'We could make a raft,' Gustaf said after a while. 'I saw two logs floating in the little bay north of where we bathed yesterday. I might find another and bind them together.'

'That would make a fine raft. I've line and hooks in my bundle. The garden has plenty of fine fat worms; no better bait anywhere.' Ernst's eyes sparkled as though his line already hung in the water.

'First we must find if there is a law,' remembered Gustaf. This was important because in Sweden he had heard many a tale of trouble when a boy fished where he shouldn't.

'No law against fishing here.' Ernst spoke with as-surance. 'This is a free country. That's the reason we came over from Sweden. Some day, Gus, I'm going to get me a farm. A real farm. Big. Sixty acres maybe, all my own. I'll have a house with three rooms. And a barn.'

'You dream big,' laughed Gustaf. 'Me, I'll have a farm, too, just large enough to make a living. Then evenings, I'll study. Uncle Axel said a boy doesn't have to be always a farmer in America. I can study and be a lawyer. Or a doctor. Or a minister or anything I want to be. *Anything*, Ernst. But I'd rather be a lawyer.'

'Who dreams big now?' laughed Ernst. 'You, a cotter's boy, a lawyer! Next you'll be writing laws or making a book!' He reached up and clung to an overhanging branch and swung himself high. 'Me, I don't want

35

to study. Too dull. I can read and figure now. Oh, I might learn some English; enough to do business. But I want to plow and sow and harvest my own land. No one can turn me off my own land.' They scrambled up the bank and around a thorn thicket.

'Aren't you glad we came over, Gus? Think of Nels, and John and Lars, back home.'

Gustaf tried to think of them, but the boys he had played with all his life seemed far away, very unreal. He hadn't thought of them for days. They ought to come to America.

Ernst and Gustaf tramped on; around the edge of the lake, along the shore. Under a great tree they stopped to wash their hands and feet and eat their bread and cheese. Ernst wanted to linger and skip stones; many tempting flat pebbles lay along the water's edge.

'I'll bet I can beat you!' he cried. 'I'll bet this goes a dozen hops.' It did. But Gustaf declined the challenge, determined to hurry on.

At the far end of the lake they came upon a group of houses, three small cabins and two good houses built with board siding and several windows. One had a wide lean-to where a smith worked great bellows at a forge.

Ernst spoke to him in Swedish. The smith answered in a loud, cordial tone and a rush of Norwegian words, that brought people running to see who had come.

'Welcome, Son. Here are some new boys!' he shouted. 'Where do you live?'

'I live with my brother and his family, in the cabin at the other end of the lake.'

'That would be Pearman's place.' The smith stopped work and wiped grimy hands on his leather apron.

'Lange must have sold it, then. Been long enough doing it! That's because the soil is too thin. Never make a go of that place farming, boys.'

Gustaf listened with amazement. What would his father think of those words? And the place so pretty and green! Likely a smith wouldn't know much about farming.

Ernst asked about the plow. Could they rent one? And for how much?

'Surely you can! A plow rents for four dollars an acre around here now. It's late for plowing or it would be five. Want it now?'

Ernst rubbed his head, puzzled. It would have been better, he thought, if Carl had come to make his own bargain.

'We haven't money to rent,' Gustaf spoke up straight-forwardly. 'Could I work to pay for renting? I could work right now. I'm strong.'

The smith pondered. He had an extra job of wheels to rim — they had really been promised for yesterday but they were not even begun. Andersen was wanting hinges for his door. He thought of half a dozen jobs he was neglecting. Gustaf watched him anxiously.

'It's a go, Son,' the smith decided. 'You start work now. I'll pay you a dollar a week; and give you dinner so you won't have to go home at noon.'

'Thank you, sir, I'll work my best. But four weeks — Father's crop ought to be in now. Could I work extra, sir, so Father could get the plow sooner?'

'You ought to make a good farmer, Son, planning well and you just a boy.' He turned to Ernst. 'Run along home and tell your brother he can have the plow and team tomorrow and get his acre in at once. And if he plows a little more'n one acre, who's to bother? Tell him his boy will be home for supper. And say,' he added as an afterthought, 'does he want a couple of piglets? Two dollars apiece? Bergensen here's got more'n he needs.'

Ernst lingered, in no hurry to take home news that Gustaf had the first job. The boy took off his blue coat, hung it on a wooden peg, and started pumping the bellows under the smith's instruction.

'Couldn't *I* get a job?' Ernst asked one of the men. I'd work hard.'

The men looked at each other uneasily. Before this new boy they would like to appear prosperous employers.

'A man from Down East — near Boston, I think it's said,' remembered one, 'has a big place north of Pearman's. Some three miles it is. He owns a lot of cattle. He sometimes hires.'

'Thank you, sir!' Ernst was willing to go, now. 'North from my brother's place, did you say?' He was careful not to repeat Pearman's name. People must learn that Carl Larsson was the owner now.

'Yes, north,' repeated the man — Nelsen, Ernst had heard him called. 'Go back the way you came. Then along the lake, north, till you come to a hill. Widow Petersson's cabin is there and Bergvaal's place just beyond. He's moving to Chicago as soon as he can sell. He's been sick and can't make a living on this thin land. Walk north to the next farm. Baker's the name. He's a good man.'

'Tell your brother to get that plow and team tomorrow,' the smith called after him. 'No use his waiting. We'll get the pay out of this bright lad here — see to that myself!' He roared with hearty laughter as he hammered out a shower of sparks on his anvil.

Ernst set off at a brisk trot. If he hurried, he might get home with the news about the plow and Gustaf's job and still have time to go to Baker's before night. He mustn't forget the pigs — Carl wanted two pigs. Whatever people meant by saying this was poor country when a person could get a job for the asking? In Sweden he might have tried for a year and got nothing. Ernst hurried on, without stopping to toss even one tempting pebble.

Carl Larsson could hardly believe the news Ernst brought.

'Gus has a job? A dollar a week?' He frowned suddenly. 'Is this a joke you play? Maybe Gus is hiding behind a tree to laugh at our easy believing?'

'It is good to make a joke, yes. This is business.' Ernst was much annoyed. He repeated what he had said. 'Gus has a job to earn the plow rent. You are to come tomorrow and get the plow and team. "If you plow a little more than one acre, who's to bother?" the smith said. Gus gets his dinner, too, and comes home before dark. And you can buy two nice little pigs — two dollars apiece, they are. Now I go and get *me* a job!' Ernst tossed his blond head boastfully. 'Of Baker. From Down East — Boston.'

'Such a country!' The mother shook her head in wonderment. 'One job and maybe another already! This is a good place, Carl.'

'The smith said ——' Ernst stopped suddenly. The

smith might not know about farming as Carl Larsson did. Why spoil a good day with word about thin soil? The garden certainly looked fine. The money was spent.

He got a drink from the well and set out north.

'Find a job for me, Ernst!' called Elna. 'I can work as hard as you can!'

'And you a girl! You should stay and help your mother.'

'You should help Father,' laughed Elna good-humoredly.

'I'll see what I can do,' promised Ernst grandly. He was in the woods by now, but the words came back clearly. Elna watched him out of sight and then went in to start supper. Gustaf would be hungry. She would like to go and see him at the forge. Once the garden was planted there would be more time. Humming happily, she measured the cereal, little suspecting what her advice to Ernst would bring.

THE COACH DRIVER

Chapter Six

GUSTAF set off for work in high spirits. He had been at his job for three weeks and he liked it better every day. The walk to the other end of the lake seemed nothing now that he was used to it. He liked the smith, and most of all he liked to hear the talk of the men who came to the smithy.

Everything at home was going well, too. The field was plowed and planted in rye and potatoes. Garden stuff was coming along fine. Berries were ripe in the woods and his mother had made a tart for supper last evening. Work was easy when a person had a stomachful of good food each night.

Usually Gustaf arrived at the smithy early enough to set the place to rights before the smith came. As he neared the place this morning he noticed that the smith was already there and he ran the last bit of the way.

'Both stages are due to be here this morning,' the smith explained. 'One from Watertown and one from Prairie du Chien. It'll be just like them to come at the same time, so we'd better be ready. Sort out the shoes,

Gus, and get a good fire going. One time last summer I had two stages here and three of the horses needing shoes. No boy to blow the bellows either. It was a hustle I'll never forget! All the passengers fussing about the delay, as though it was anyone's fault and me working like a fool to please 'em!'

Gustaf hung up his coat and went to work. Soon the forge was tidied; iron horseshoes taken down yesterday were sorted as to size and hung overhead. The fire blazed, ready to blow to white heat on a minute's notice. Yesterday's litter from a wheel-rimming job was cleared away and a bucket of fresh water and a dipper set by the wide doorway.

'You're looking pretty fine these days, Gus.' The smith had time for talk now that he was ready. 'Like America?'

'Oh, yes, sir! We like it fine! Everything goes with good luck since we came.'

'Did the other boy get that job? I always meant to ask you.'

'My father's brother? Yes, sir. He got it that same evening. He went over right away to see Mr. Baker as Mr. Nelsen told him to. And he got the job. My sister has a place, too.'

'Your sister!' exclaimed the smith. 'How old is she?' He sat on a stump chair and lighted his pipe.

'My sister is only eight,' Gustaf replied, 'but Mr. Baker told Ernst about the Swedish family who needed help; Bergvaal is the name. They live north, on the way to Mr. Baker's place.'

'I know him. He has the hurt leg.'

'Yes, sir. Well, Mrs. Bergvaal needed help the worst

42

way. My mother couldn't be spared at home, so Elna goes over every morning with Ernst. She tends the baby and helps with the fire and in the garden; she's very handy. Mrs. Bergvaal pays her twenty cents each week and some flour and garden stuff,' Gustaf added proudly. 'New carrots and beets taste good, and ours were put in late, you know. Yesterday they sent us some corn to grind for cakes. It tasted fine. Yes, we're lucky, sir. Father says that with three working we may be able to buy a plow and an ox by spring. My sister learns, too.' Now that Gustaf had such an interested listener he found much to say. 'Mrs. Bergvaal speaks some English and she knows a lot of American ways. They've been over six years, she says. Elna teaches us new words each evening.'

'You want to learn English?'

'Oh, yes, sir. I want to speak it and read it. But how to begin learning to read English, I don't yet know.'

'I wouldn't be bothered with learning English, myself,' said the smith. 'There are plenty of people around here who speak a Scandinavian language. And more will be coming over every year — you'll see!'

'All the more reason to know English,' Gustaf answered. 'I may be wrong, sir, but I figure that all those people will be wanting to do business and learn American ways. They'll be glad to know a Swede who can talk for them here.' The smith pondered.

'It does make some sense. Have you books to study?'

'No, sir, and I wish I had. I'd like to see how English words look on a page.'

Gustaf took out his pocketknife and set to whittling. The great doors of the smithy flapped gently in the morning breeze and he made a new wedge to hold the south one open. The smith puffed clouds of smoke from his corncob pipe while he did this unusual business of hard thinking.

'You tell the coach driver what you want — the one from Watertown. He's a funny fellow. Interested in everything. Once in a while a passenger leaves a paper in his coach, careless like. I've seen 'em. Perhaps he will give you the next one he gets. It does no harm to ask. Well, they'll be coming soon. Better get the fire going, Gus.'

Gustaf jumped for the bellows, his mind a whirl of new ideas. Suppose he should get a paper for his very own — a wild notion, but just suppose. He could take it home and study it. He could copy the letters and make words to look just like those printed on the paper. But what could he write on? As he worked the bellows, he turned the matter over in his mind. Might as well figure it out just in case he *did* get a paper.

A coach pulled in shortly, one horse limping, a stone caught in his shoe. Gustaf ran out to help unhitch and bring in the horse. Fretful passengers climbed out to stretch themselves with a stroll or to rest under the trees. This delay was disappointing. Now they couldn't get to Milwaukee till late, for all their early start.

But the smith was a master hand with horses. In record time the old shoe was taken off, the stone removed, and the bruised hoof treated. Then a new shoe fitted neatly.

'Give him a little water, Gus. Only a little, mind! Can't water a horse too much when he's just starting out. We'll let him rest half an hour and then he'll be good as new. That's the driver I was telling you about — did you ask him?'

The driver came into the smithy to inquire about his horse. It kept him busy trying to humor his passengers and keep track of his horse at the same time. And now a cloud of dust to the west showed the coach from Prairie du Chien was coming. He wished he could get away before that arrival — two coaches always delayed each other.

'Nearly ready now?' he asked. 'They all seem in a worse hurry than usual today. Travelers are always rushing. "Can't you go faster?" they ask me. Just as though there wasn't another day coming.' He put a fresh wad of tobacco in his cheek and grinned at Gustaf good-naturedly. He went by twice each week and he had noticed the new boy.

'How do you like your job, Son?'

'Fine, sir,' Gustaf replied. 'I wonder, sir . . .' then he stopped. It seemed like a good deal to ask of a stranger to borrow a valuable thing like a newspaper.

'He's got reading on his mind,' the smith explained, as he patted the horse's head. 'Swedish isn't good enough for him now that he's come to the United States. He wants to speak English and read it, too. As though knowing one language wasn't enough for anyone!'

'Oh, I don't know.' The driver looked at Gustaf with new interest. 'I don't care for reading myself, but they do say there's a lot to be learned from books. Sure, I'll give you a paper, Son. I've got one right now on the coach box. It's a Madison paper. A man was reading it yesterday and telling me that there's a new society for learning how to farm. Your father'll think that's a good joke — a newspaper telling a man how to farm!' He slapped his side and roared with laughter.

'Come! We'll get it now.' Gustaf followed him to the coach and watched as he lifted the folded blanket on which he sat and drew from under it a single-sheet newspaper. He spread it out for Gustaf to see.

'Here it tells about the farm society — agricultural, they call it, stylish-like. And here's about the train to Chicago. Some think I should be worried about trains taking my business. But I'm not. Fools may ride on trains but sensible folk will always take a stagecoach. Gets there surely and no smoke or noise. You'll find a lot to read about once you get on to the words.'

'Thank you, sir.' Gustaf took the paper carefully, looking at the strange combinations of letters that danced before his eyes in the hot July sunshine.

'Know anyone who can tell you the words?' asked the driver.

'No. But I'll find someone. I can copy the letters and get used to the words by myself. Then, once I know the meaning, it will be easy.'

'Make a log slate, Son.' One of the passengers had noticed the talk and spoke up. 'I know a man who learned English that way. Get a basswood log if you can. Ash will do, too. Split it in half and smooth it. You can make good letters with a nail. I used to watch him do it. But I wouldn't be bothered myself. Too much work.'

'The log is a good idea, sir, and I thank you,' said Gustaf. 'I'll do it evenings.'

'I'll give him the nail,' said the smith, not to be outdone by others in helping his own boy. 'You can take two with you tonight, Gus. The horse is ready now,

46

driver. No hurry. Glad to have you stay as long as you like. The other coach will be coming.'

Gustaf led the horse out and helped to hitch. The passengers hurried to their seats, anxious to be gone. The driver flourished his whip noisily. They were off.

Gustaf watched them around the bend of the road. Then he looked at the paper in his hand. So much to happen in a few minutes. Now he could look at English words. The next thing was to find out what those words meant. He folded the paper neatly and put it in his pocket, quickly, before the other coach arrived.

CHANGES BREWING

Chapter Seven

GUSTAF could hardly get home fast enough that evening. Wouldn't the family be amazed to see a newspaper printed in English? His very own, too! And two nails so bright and shining. Sharp, fine for pencils. They would make an even line on soft wood.

But nearing home, *he* was surprised, too. He sniffed happily — plum jam! His mother was cooking his favorite plum jam. The pungent fragrance was exciting.

Elna ran to meet him. 'You'll never guess what we are going to have, Gus!'

'Oh, wouldn't I? Think I don't know plum jam when I smell it?'

CHANGES BREWING

'Oh, that!' Elna dismissed plum jam with a laugh.
'You knew the plums were ripening. Mother made a
tasty jam — even without sugar. But there's a real surprise. Mrs. Bergvaal sent Mother yeast and a rule for
making light bread. Mrs. Baker gave it to her and she
shared it. She had me bring it over this morning. The
bread looks wonderful, Gus. Hans caught fish, too.
That raft you made works fine. It's so steady he can fish
by himself. Ernst is just home. Better hurry and wash,
Gus. Supper's nearly ready.' Elna missed her brother
now that they worked at different places. She loved to
meet him and report on the day's doings.

By the time the boys had had a swim, the supper cloth
was spread on the grass and the food brought out.
Broiled fish, greens, light bread, very tasty and delicious, the new jam, and milk — a real feast, the best
meal they had had in many years.

'We eat like lords,' said Larsson. 'You are lucky to
have a job with Mrs. Bergvaal, Elna. This bread is good.'

'I've a start of yeast left over, as she told me. I keep
it on the shelf your father made me in the well,' the
mother explained to Gustaf. 'You boys should make us
spoons so we can all eat at once the American way.
Your father is planning a table, and when we each have
a spoon and bowl it will be nice.'

Gustaf listened. So much was happening this evening.
Would this be the time to bring out his paper? Or should
he wait? Daylight was best for showing it.

'Do you like your supper, Gus?' asked the mother.
He ate well but seemed quiet and thoughtful.

'Oh, yes, Mother! You made it fine! It's a celebration, though you didn't know that.'

'A celebration?'

'Yes. I'm starting to learn English.' He paused to relish their amazement. 'The coach driver gave me a paper this morning.' He pulled it out of his pocket and carefully spread it on the clean grass. 'It's printed in Madison, the state capitol of Wisconsin. The smith gave me nails for pencils and I'm going to make a log slate for writing my lessons.'

They stared at the paper and nails, too amazed for words.

'What's a log slate?' Hans broke the silence to ask.

'A split log. A passenger on the coach gave me the idea. I'll smooth it and then press marks with the nail for letters. When I have it full with one lesson, I'll learn that, then dress it down for the next.'

'Do you know any of the words, Gus?' Larsson looked from the paper to his son.

'No. But I can learn to print the words. Some day I'll learn the meaning.'

'Mrs. Bergvaal knows English words,' said Elna. 'I'll take the paper to her and she can tell me. Maybe some day when Mr. Bergvaal gets better she can come over and see your log slate.'

'You would have to be very careful of the paper, Elna,' said Gustaf. Much as he wanted to know the meaning of those words, he doubted the wisdom of letting Elna carry the paper through the woods.

'Careful!' cried Elna. 'I'll be as careful as you could be, Gus.'

'Then take it tomorrow, Elna. And be sure you listen and get it right when she tells you.'

'Better wrap the paper in a fold of linen, Daughter,' suggested the mother. 'Then you will not spoil it with

50

warm fingers. I'd be right proud to have you read and write English, Gus.'

'Let's split a log now,' said the father, standing up briskly, tiredness forgotten. 'There will be light for a while yet. I want to get at that table your mother is talking about, anyway. I'll need three lengths of log for that. You may have the fourth for your slate, Gus. I'll dress it down for you.'

'Then you'll make the table; days are getting shorter. It will be nice to have a table in the house.' The mother smiled at them all happily.

'I'll make log seats,' said the father. 'I came across a log yesterday. It's been down a year or more and is well seasoned. I'll saw it up. You boys can whittle spoons. I may go to Watertown soon and get salt and other things. A salt bucket's a good thing to lay a tallow-soaked rag on till we get time to make candles. We'll be needing light for all this evening work we aim to do.'

Gustaf folded the paper tenderly, carried it into the cabin, and put it under the brass box on the shelf. That box was getting heavier now that Elna and Ernst put their wages in there each week. The plow rent would be worked out in another week and then Gus, too, would have money for the box. He went out to the woodpile to help his father.

Mrs. Bergvaal could read English fairly well and when Elna brought the newspaper to her, she carefully made a list of Swedish words to tell the meaning. Each evening Gustaf learned five new words by printing them on the log. It was a proud moment when he had learned enough words to read about the train to Chicago, the Methodist Church, and the arrivals in the state capitol.

THEY CAME FROM SWEDEN

Soon Mr. Bergvaal was better and Elna's job ended. That was fine for him, but Elna missed the company, and often went over to help in a neighborly way even though there was plenty for her to do at home. The garden must be weeded often and ripe vegetables gathered. She and Hans picked berries in the woods — raspberries, black and red, luscious blackberries and elderberries which the mother made into a tasty drink.

Mrs. Baker sent over two hanks of wool by Ernst and promised more if Mrs. Larsson would help with the cooking at harvest-time. So Gustaf set up the loom by the fireplace and the spinning wheel in the corner. Hans learned to card wool, and as the evenings were cooler the whole family worked in the little cabin.

One afternoon in early September the mother had just finished a big washing. The boy's coats got very soiled working as they did. Gustaf's things had very hard wear at the smithy and would need a lot of mending. She had just spread his coat on the table to see how to repair it when Mrs. Bergvaal arrived with news. They had sold their place and were moving! The widow Petersson had sold, too.

'Who is it buys?' the mother asked. Gustaf would be very disappointed to have Mrs. Bergvaal move away, for he was doing finely with her help in English.

'Oh, it's just business,' Mrs. Bergvaal replied easily. "I do not understand it either. Someone in Chicago thinks my place is good — though he has never seen it. He has Lange buy and says he can sell it tomorrow for twice the money. We are glad, for my man's leg does not get strong and we are tired of farming. We have kinfolk in Chicago.'

'We have kin there, too,' Mrs. Larsson said proudly.
'Wait! I'll get the paper with Axel's numbers. See where
he lives?' She spread out the folded slip beside the pile
of clean clothes. 'If you see him, tell him we do well.'
Then she stirred the fire to heat the coffee and set out rye
cakes.

'Gus says it is a long way to Chicago,' remarked Elna

'We travel by train. All the way from Janesville.'
Mrs. Bergvaal's eyes sparkled gleefully. She knew this
was an astonishing bit of news.

'The steam train!' Elna, Hans, the mother could
hardly believe.

'Aye, the steam train,' repeated the visitor, relishing
their amazement. 'We go to Watertown and sell the cow
and ox. That's out of the way, but Lange is there. He
drives us to Janesville, where the train starts. I never
thought to ride on a train,' she admitted as she sipped the
coffee. 'Never. It goes quickly. We are in Chicago that
night. Like magic.'

'It costs dear,' remembered the mother. Gustaf had
read about it just last evening.

'Aye, but we sold the place. My man has a job ready
for him in Chicago making cabinets for a builder there.
He is to work only twelve hours a day and Sundays off.
This is a great country.' She was so excited and happy
she had no thought for the people who were staying on a
farm. Now there would be no one to understand Swedish
or talk of the old country. Mrs. Larsson bade her good-
bye reluctantly.

The Bergvaals were not the only ones leaving, either.
Every day, at the smithy, Gustaf was hearing talk about
leaving Wisconsin. Herr Lange had opened a general

store in Watertown, and when Larsson went over for supplies Lange would talk about nothing but selling land.

'Why not sell and go West?' he asked Larsson. 'You can make money easy as anything.' Larsson was really annoyed. Did Lange think that making money was everything? The Larssons wanted a *home*. Lange talked and talked. He sent a sack of candy to the children, lemon drops that melted in the mouth with a sweet sour taste, very delicious. The children hoped their father would go to Watertown again, but he avoided it. Surely Minnesota Territory, Lange talked of, could be no better than Wisconsin. It was all very disturbing. But for Gustaf, the mother would have been even more disturbed.

Gus liked his job. He could read most of the paper now and had a new sheet the coach driver saved for him. A lucky thing *that* was for the first paper was about worn out. The smith was so proud that he invited people to come and hear Gustaf read news. This brought good business to the smithy and he raised Gustaf's wages twenty-five cents a week. Yes, Gustaf had reason to be happy.

Chapter Eight

ONE evening early in the autumn, Gustaf hurried home with news.

'Pastor Håkansson is to be in Watertown Sunday. There will be church.'

His mother stepped to the door to see if she heard rightly.

'Church, Gus? Real church?'

'Yes, the smith said so. We are all to come. He and the others are going.'

'They are Norwegian,' the mother remembered.

'Yes, but Lutheran. It makes no difference here; I asked the smith.'

'Where will the service be?' Elna asked.

'In Swansson's house. The women are scrubbing it. May we go, Mother? It's the first service here in six months — and only eight miles.'

'Go?' The mother was astonished at the question. 'Of course we'll go. Though two days is little enough time for getting ready. We must do your father credit and not look like cotters.'

Larsson laughed. 'They'll think I'm lucky with a family like mine — all well and strong as you are!'

Mrs. Larsson began planning. Rye cakes, flat and well baked, were strung on a pole near the roof. Hans could catch fish, they were biting well now. If she could only bake some cakes — nut cakes would be fine.

'Gus, you and Ernst gather up your clothes tonight. Elna and I shall rise before the sun tomorrow and wash. Next we'll dig the potatoes — there's a feel of frost in the air and we must not risk losing them. Then if you and Hans could find some nuts ——'

'Oh, we can, Mother! We'll find so many you can't use them all.' Her mother laughed at such a silly notion.

'You'll have to be up early to do that!' And Hans and Elna had gone to bed willingly. Next morning, as soon as the washing was finished they started for the woods, carrying the willow baskets Gustaf had made for them.

'Go to the top of the hill between the two lakes, Pine and Beaver,' Ernst had said, and he should know, for he often walked in that direction.

Elna looked down the slope toward Beaver Lake. Tall pines towered there, and the ground was soft with pine needles. But there were no nuts. To the east, maples flamed red and gold; to the southwest, down the steep hill toward Pine Lake sumac bushes were crimson.

'There's a good Christmas tree, Sister.' Hans pointed to a small, perfectly shaped spruce near-by.

'Oh, Hans, how beautiful it is! We must show it to

56

Father. It's good luck to find the tree before snow. Perhaps we can find some berries to string. If Gus makes the candle moulds as he plans, it will be perfect.' They walked round and round the little tree admiring it and planning. Suddenly Elna remembered their errand.

'It is truly a fine tree. But looking at it gets us no nuts. Maybe Ernst meant nearer Beaver Lake. That looks like a butternut tree down there. Remember that good butternut cake Ernst brought from Mrs. Baker's? But the hulls stain. We must be careful.'

Sliding, slipping, the children barely stopped by the water's edge. And it *was* a butternut tree, with more nuts than they could carry on several trips. They filled their baskets and hurried home.

'First spread them out to dry,' said the mother, when she had admired them. 'Down by the lake — no. They'd not dry overnight, there.'

'Put them on the hearth,' suggested the father, who was working by the shed.

'Yes, and dirty my clean hearth with dark juice! I guess by the lake is best.'

But when Gustaf came home for supper, the nuts hadn't dried a bit.

'I'll fix them,' he said quickly. 'There's that log I split last night. I'll lay it on the hearth and the nuts on it. With a good backlog to keep the fire going all night, they'll be dry by morning.'

'You've a good head, Gus, like my father, Gustaf Anders,' approved the mother. So the nuts were dried and the cakes made the next day.

Late Saturday afternoon, Gustaf asked Hans, 'Do you have your lesson for tomorrow?'

THEY CAME FROM SWEDEN

'Will there be Sunday School?'

'The smith wasn't sure. But you can be ready. I'll help you.'

Hans ran for his A.B.C. book and began reviewing. Had they stayed in Sweden he would have known but a few pages. But hours on the long journey his mother had taught him. Gustaf and Elna had repeated with him whole pages. Now he opened the book and looked at the picture of the crowing rooster on the first page. Underneath was a verse saying, 'If you learn your lesson well, the rooster will bring you a penny.' At home, he used to put the book by his bed Saturday night and in the morning a penny was on the rooster.

As Hans scrubbed in the tub before the fire that evening he said questions and answers. He patted himself dry to the rhythm of a psalm and when he recited it all for Gustaf, every word was perfect.

'Now shall I have a penny in the morning, Gus?'

'Wait and see! How do I know what the rooster does in America?' Gustaf answered.

Hans looked from Gustaf to his mother, to his father. It was a puzzle how a penny got into the book. He pulled out the trundle bed and snuggled under the cover, the book handy on the floor near his head. As Hans dozed off, Gustaf reached into his pocket and took out something which he held in his half open fist to show his mother.

Sunday morning breakfast was a hasty meal and the mother set to work packing the fine dinner in bundles. Hans wakened with the stir and shyly reached for his book. There right on the rooster was a bright, new United States penny. He jumped up and ran to show

Gustaf the coin; Gustaf was *very* surprised; no one else had time to look. Elna was down at the cove admiring her new bonnet, its red-and-green embroidery matching her striped petticoat. Gustaf then brought wood ready for their return; he brushed himself off and put on his blue coat. It was clean, but much too small. His arms hung long below the sleeves. Friends in Sweden would hardly have known him, he had grown so tall. And his arms were strong from working the bellows. He looked ruefully at his hands.

'Is the coat short or are the arms long, Mother?' he asked. 'Never mind, the smith has good business now and promises me another raise before Christmas.' He fastened the latch and they set out.

About a mile from Watertown, the Larssons stopped by a creek to wash their feet and put on wooden shoes. One couldn't, of course, waste good shoes wearing them to walk across country. Swansson's house was crowded when they arrived, but room was made for Elna and her mother on the women's side and for the others with the men.

Pastor preached from the Scriptures for two hours. Hans went to sleep against Gustaf, and didn't awaken till they all stood up to sing the old hymn of the Reformation, 'A Mighty Fortress Is Our God,' at the end.

After dinner, eaten on the grass in front of the house, children began to play together, women made the place tidy, men gathered to talk business, and the older boys wandered off to the grove close by, little boys following till the pastor should call them for Sunday School.

Ernst and Gustaf followed the youths, though they lagged a bit, suddenly shy as they saw that most of the others were already acquainted. One of the boys, a tall, thick-set lad, turned and saw them.

'Want to fight and prove your worth?' he cried, taking a stance and sparring with his fists in Gustaf's direction.

Gustaf knew the phrase well enough. Every new boy had to go through that sort of initiation in school at home. But he had no desire to fight at this time and place.

'Why don't you lick him?' whispered Ernst, with so little movement of his lips no one but Gustaf suspected he had spoken. 'I'll wager on you to match him. He doesn't work at a smithy. Look at his soft arms.' Gustaf had already sized that point up and had great confidence, too, in his own strength. But this was the Sabbath . . .

'I'll fight if you can match this!' he answered in a firm, cheerful voice. And quick as a flash he bent down to roll a cartwheel — one, in perfect form. Two. Three. Four and five. He came up on his feet steadily, with a grin, as he tossed back his hair and paused in the middle of the astonished group, for the other boy to take his turn.

'Do it again!' cried little boys who had chanced to watch.

'Where did you learn that?' demanded one of the older lads.

'Poof! That's nothing!' The tall boy didn't like to lose the limelight he had gained by his bold challenge to the new boy. 'Anyone can do that.'

'Of course,' agreed Gustaf cheerfully. 'Let's see you!'

'You know you can't,' said half a dozen voices.

'Who wants to?' demanded the boy. 'Let him fight, as I said.'

'When you match my cartwheels,' said Gustaf, stand-

60

ing comfortably without panting after his feat, his voice cheerful but firm.

Forced by the eyes of the crowd to try, the tall boy attempted one, two, and toppled over, his balance lost along with his pride.

'Do it again, Gus!' cried one of the younger boys. He had asked Ernst for the new boy's name.

Obligingly Gustaf turned his wheels again, this time reversing the direction and landing at the edge of the grove — just as the pastor came for a chat with the boys.

'Good work, my boy,' he approved. 'Where did you learn that trick?'

'I learned cartwheels in Sweden, but I practiced at noon at the smithy. Sometimes I did eight at a time and that pleased the smith.'

'And how came you to show your skill now?'

A half-dozen boys spoke up to explain the challenge and Gustaf's answer.

The pastor laughed when he heard the tale.

'To use your wits is better than to fight any day, Sabbath or not. What's your name?' he asked the tall boy.

'Axel Bergson.'

'What do you do, Axel?'

'I help my father. As soon as he can spare me, I'll work on the railroad.'

'That's good. We need railroads. But remember, today, it is better to use your wits than to pick a quarrel. Railroad men are pretty good fighters. I want you back here with a whole nose!'

'Your name, son?' he asked of Gustaf.

'Gustaf Larsson, sir.'

'He learns English in a paper' — one of the boys who

had this bit from Ernst spoke up before the pastor could question further.

'You do? That's not easy when there is no school.' He got the story from Gustaf of the newspaper and the log and nail and asked him some questions in English. 'Come with me now and I'll give you a book with Swedish and English words, both. You'll like it. And you can return it to me when I come in the spring.'

Gustaf promised gratefully. He studied the little book evenings during the winter. But he never saw the good pastor again.

CHRISTMAS, 1856

Chapter Nine

'QUICK, Hans! Now we can clean the house and surprise Mother.'

'Do you know how, Elna?'

'Of course, silly!' Elna peered from the crack in the door to make sure her mother was out of hearing. 'She will be gone till dark. If Mrs. Baker likes the weaving and makes coffee for her, she will be away three hours, plenty of time for us. We'll begin by the fireplace. I made new brushes, stiff and strong, and Mother doesn't even guess I have them.' Elna dashed out of the door and ran along the deeply trodden path through the snow. Hidden in the woodpile were the two new brushes, the twigs well selected and firmly tied. No wonder Elna was proud of making them. Back in the cabin, she poured hot water into a small tub, refilled the kettle, and swung the crane over the fire.

'Should I begin at the top, Hans, or at the bottom?'

Hans tried to look wise but couldn't answer.

'Mother is ever saying she wishes these walls were clean. Now they will be fine. I'll start at the top and work down.' She shook the brush in the water, climbed on the edge of the post bed, and began to scrub. But the more she scrubbed the dirtier the water got; the more water she used, the more dirt; soon the whole wall was covered with thick, blackish mud. Elna was beside herself with worry. What *would* her mother say? What *could* she do?

As for Hans, he never had bothered about the dirty wall, but now Elna was crying; really crying, though she rubbed her sleeve across her eyes and tried to pretend it was only the smoke from the fireplace. He *must* do something!

'Look, Sister! You have made a window. Mother will like that, for we need more light.' Wondering, Elna wiped her eyes and looked. Daylight came through a crack and the wind blew with a chill draft. She stared in silent misery at the result of her work.

'Up Swedes for King and countrymen!' Loud singing outside interrupted the silence in the cabin.

'It's Gus!' Elna jumped off the bed and ran to the door. 'It isn't time for him yet!' But there he was, coming around the end of the lake.

'Gus will know what to do,' said Hans, and they ran to meet him.

'Hello!' Gustaf greeted them. 'I had to deliver a horse for the smith, so I'm early.'

'Oh, Gus, I'm glad you came!' Elna ran and grabbed his sleeve. 'I was scrubbing the wall to make it clean for Christmas. And there came a hole. Whatever will Mother say!'

Gustaf hurried into the cabin, his singing stopped short.

'But you can fix it, Gus.' Hans continued hopeful though the hole was very big.

'First we shall look at it, Hans.' Gustaf climbed on the bed to look. Riverlets of mud were oozing down, making a growing hole in the wall and a wet puddle on the floor.

'To have a clean face is good, Elna, and clean dishes and beds. But this cabin is plastered with mud. If you scrub dried mud — well, it is mud. Didn't you know that that is why Mother never washed the wall? Now, we shall throw out the water and sop up the floor. I'll get a stick and scrape it. Then I'll get some earth — but the earth is frozen.'

Elna looked so discouraged he had to laugh.

'It is not bad as that, Sister. Smile a little. There will still be Christmas. You didn't get the sugar cakes wet nor the pudding. Are you a baby?' That made Elna laugh and they set to work.

They scraped the floor and pounded it hard. From the hill where the wind had blown the snow thin Gustaf fetched a couple of clods of earth. He warmed these at the hearth and watered them just a little, enough to work the dirt and paste it into the cracks.

65

'This isn't the best stuff for a wall. Come spring we'll get clay from the bank Father found by Beaver Lake. But this is as good as it was before. There now, we're going to get the tree.'

'The Christmas tree, Gus?' Hans could hardly believe.

'The Christmas tree. Father'll not be home until late. He is working on the plowshare the smith lets him make at the forge. He said we should get the tree. I'm to take his axe.' Such a nice ending to a bad afternoon! Elna jerked down their wraps from the wooden peg, warm mittens and scarves, for the day was cold, and they set out.

'Remember when we got the tree last year?' Gustaf remarked. 'John fell into the great snowbank. They'll be getting a tree from that woods today — and we are in America.'

'You should write to him. Maybe they could come here. John's father is but a poor cotter, and our father owns a farm and cabin.'

'Maybe we'll sell this and move to Minnesota Territory and have a *real* farm.'

'Ten acres is real, Gus,' said Hans, running to keep up.

'A hundred and sixty acres makes a farm in Minnesota Territory.'

'You talk big,' reproved Elna. 'Father couldn't get a hundred and sixty acres. That is for a lord.'

'Yes, he could,' insisted Gustaf, 'in Minnesota. He could homestead it. While I help shoe the horses I listen to the men talk. "There's room for all," they say. And never a word about a lord.'

'There's the tree, Gus,' interrupted Hans. 'Is it a good choice?'

CHRISTMAS, 1856

'A beauty! Couldn't pick a better if we hunted all day! Stand away! Here goes!'

By the time the tree was down, the sun set in a mass of low crimson clouds and stars began to sparkle faintly in the east. Mrs. Larsson came through the woods and heard the children. She had enjoyed hot coffee and a friendly visit; it had been a good day. Elna ran to tell her about the cleaning failure and how Gustaf had repaired the damage.

'You meant to be helpful, Daughter,' the mother said as she drew Elna toward her kindly. 'But next time let the idea be the surprise and ask me if it's best. Now let's forget it and sing while we carry the Yule tree. After your father gets home, we'll sing the evening psalm and he'll stand the tree in the cabin.'

After supper the Larsson family settled down to work before the fire. Father finished carving a small wooden pig. Mother knitted mittens. Hans strung hawberries on a fishline. Elna finished a sock she was making for her father. He would be proud to see how skillfully she had learned to toe off. Ernst whittled a willow flute. Gustaf finished a set of hanging shelves for his mother. The room steamed warmly with the freshly washed clothes drying in the darkest corner. Talk turned to last Christmas.

'Will Grandmother miss us?' asked Elna, smoothing her knitting deftly. 'Remember the cakes we made at her house last year?'

'Mother has made sugar cookies here,' said Hans. 'With nuts in them.'

'I like your ginger cookies best,' said Gustaf. 'They look grand, Mother, with store currants for eyes the way you made them.'

67

'Do you suppose my father and mother will come to America some day, Carl?' asked Mrs. Larsson. 'They are not too old for the journey.'

'Your sister Greta could come with them,' said Ernst. He often thought of pretty Greta, her yellow braids, blue eyes, and smiling mouth. 'You should write to her, Anna Marie.'

'I can give the letter to the stage driver,' said Gustaf. 'He'll like that. Carrying letters gives him more money.'

'If Grandmother Anders was here now she would tell me a story of the Yule Buck.' Hans's eyes were drooping sleepily. 'Can you tell it, Mother?'

'Aye, son. You know she always told it to Greta and me.' The mother laid her knitting aside and lifted tired Hans to her lap. The others worked on quietly.

'Once upon a time there came a night when a star shone in the east. While shepherds watched their flocks at night a great peace came over the land and all living creatures were kind each to the other.'

'That's the reason we shall put up a sheaf of rye for the birds tomorrow,' Hans sat up straight to interrupt.

'Yes, Son, because of that long-ago night, the Holy Night.

'In a cave on the mountain, two little children of a shepherd slept. They were weary from long tramping the hills with their father. Now he had to leave them awhile. So he called a great buck to him and said, "For a few hours I must go away. You shall guard my little ones. They sleep soft on the hay. Do not let any creature take it from them." Grudgingly the buck promised.

'But as soon as the shepherd was gone, the buck said to himself, "How silly for children to sleep on hay when

68

I should like some to eat. I'll take a wisp." So he took a little hay; and then a little more; and more. When the shepherd returned, the hay was gone. The children lay on cold, hard stone.

' "Cruel buck!" cried the shepherd. "Know you not that this is the Holy Night? You of all living creatures have been unkind. The lion has shut his mouth. The hyena has stilled his growl. Even the spider left off weaving his web. But you ate the children's straw. I shall cast a spell over you! From this night on, every year on Holy Night you shall roam through the world trying to do a kindness to a child. And no one shall know you or thank you and so the spell shall never be broken." '

Hans sighed, his eyes starry in the firelight.

'Maybe the Yule Buck will come to Wisconsin. He came to Grandmother's in Sweden.'

'You'll have to go to sleep quickly, then, for he never comes to boys who sit up late,' said Gustaf. 'That's what I learned one night when I sat up to watch for him.' So Hans undressed and climbed into the trundle bed. And in no time at all, it seemed, it was morning of the day before Christmas.

This day, Wednesday, there was no sun and the wind was colder. In the afternoon Elna and Hans put on their warmest clothes and went with their father to get spruce. He cut armfuls of small branches and they spread them before the door of the cabin and stamped them firmly. When the door was opened a sweet, spicy odor filled the little room with Christmas fragrance.

'I wish there was *Julotta*, Mother,' said Elna. 'Remember how we got up at four last year and Father pulled us on the sled to the five-o'clock service?'

'Some day there will be church here and we'll go to the Christmas service. We'll read the Bible and Psalms tomorrow anyway. The kettle is hot, now, we must begin the baths. Your turn first, Elna.'

Dark came early under lowering skies. As soon as Gustaf got home, Larsson dropped the bar across the door to stop its rattling and the mother hung a shawl across the west window.

'Now we can trim the tree!' cried Hans.

'First the strings of berries,' said Elna. 'You made them nice, Hans.' He grinned happily as she draped them across the tree. 'Now the yarn.' All fall as yarn was spun and dyed, as clothes were made or mended, the children had treasured scraps. Mostly they were dark bits, but a few were bright and gay, for the mother was clever with the dye pot. Elna dropped these bits on the tree, making flecks of color. Larsson himself put the candles on last, the best of the five at the top. He made them stand straight and firm. Gustaf, the tallest child, lighted them with a brand from the fireplace. His hand was steady, but his eyes danced with excitement as he stood on a log chair for reaching the topmost candle.

'Now we'll sing all the Christmas songs,' said the mother.

The presents were wonderful. Hans thought he had never seen such a fine toy as his pig. Gustaf played a Christmas tune on his flute. Elna hung a tiny wooden locket on a bit of yarn and put it around her neck. The mother dished up the supper and they sat at table to eat, like ladies and gentlemen. There was pork, smoked and tasty, clabber cheese, hot potato soup, plum jam, *limpa* (a sweet Swedish rye bread), and Christmas cookies — a wonderful meal. They ate till they were too full to sing. The father went to bed Blossom for the night. Inside the cabin was warmth and light. Outside the wind howled; clouds hid the Christmas stars.

Chapter Ten

THE storm lasted three days, blowing snow into cracks, filling the air like a curtain. Fortunately there was wood stacked by the cabin, so the Larssons kept fairly warm. The path to Blossom's shed was dug freshly every hour so she could be fed and milked. It was lucky, too, that clothes had been washed and food baked for Christmas.

The first morning after Christmas, Gustaf was as restless as a grasshopper in August. He fiddled around at this and that, never still a minute.

'What ails you, Gus, to act like this?' his father finally said. 'The cabin is not over large at best, and with you moving around all the time we're crowded.'

'I ought to be off to the smithy, Father!'

'We should all be at work. But with this storm you'd

72

be lost before you got to the end of the lake. The smith will not look for you.'

'He won't have any horses brought in to shoe, anyway,' said Ernst.

'That's why I want to be there,' Gustaf answered. 'He's showing me how to make a door latch for Mrs. Nelsen and we could work on it if no one came in. She wants it now.'

'Well, you can't go, Son' — his father's voice was firm. 'You might as well make yourself happy here. Get out your knife and whittle your mother a pair of spoons. I've the wood ready. She needs more and it will keep you from fretting.' So Gustaf got out his knife and went to work.

At noon the fourth day clouds cleared away and the sun shone brilliantly. Gustaf had contrived some crude snowshoes, and on these he set out for the smithy. Ernst left for the Bakers' and the others began to work at accumulated chores. Ashes were carried from the fireplace and dumped into the ash pit for soap-making in the spring. Blossom's shed got a cleaning. Larsson dug a path to the well and Elna and the mother drew water. The supply in the cabin was gone.

Early in the afternoon as Mrs. Larsson worked alone in the cabin, someone knocked loudly at the door.

'Come!' she called gaily. Perhaps Hans was making a little joke.

The door swung open. It was Herr Lange. He stamped his feet free of snow and rubbed his cold hands.

'Is your husband here?'

'Yes, Herr Lange, I'll call him. But come to the fire and make yourself warm.' She hurried outside and

73

called. Larsson came at once. What in the world could Herr Lange want important enough to bring him here in all this snow?

'I've an offer for your place, Larsson,' began Lange. 'I told you I would.'

'My place!' Larsson was astonished. 'No one has been to see it. Who wants it?'

'A Chicago agent. He knows land around about here. He came up once. He makes you an offer.'

'What will he pay?' Elna and Hans came in with armfuls of wood. Pay for what? they wondered.

'Two hundred cash as soon as the papers are signed. With that in your pocket, Larsson, you can go to Minnesota Territory, take up a homestead claim, and have a *real* farm to be proud of. Others are doing it.'

'I may not want to sell,' objected Larsson stubbornly. He had thought much about this idea since Bergvaal left; Sunday in Watertown he had talked with men after church. But he liked his place; Ernst and Gustaf had good jobs and they were all happy. Minnesota Territory seemed far away. Lange talked on.

'You can move out in March while the snow lasts. Take your goods by sled. Get to the Mississippi River by the time traffic opens; go up by boat, cheap. Railroads will be through from Milwaukee to Prairie du Chien come summer, but that's a costly way for a man with a family to travel. Sled and boat is better. Get there in time to put a crop in.

'Minnesota shipped two thousand bushels of wheat down the river last harvest and there'll be ten times that next fall. You can get good wheat land out there for a dollar and twenty-five an acre.'

Mrs. Larsson thought the man would never stop talking! Who wanted to sell her home and move in the dead of winter? Not she! The coffee boiled up; she poured a cupful and set rye cakes and cheese on the table for Herr Lange.

Soon the price was raised to two hundred and twenty-five dollars, and finally Larsson agreed to sell for two hundred and forty dollars — more money than he had ever had; two hundred dollars more than he had paid for the place last June. Lange counted out fifty dollars; the rest would be paid when the papers were signed in Watertown. Mrs. Larsson filled his cup again; Lange drank it and hurried away.

'Does that mean we are going to move right now, Father?' Elna asked as the door closed. Larsson looked at her abstractedly, without answering.

Mrs. Larsson sat on her stool by the fireplace and folded her hands under her gray apron. 'If the place is worth two hundred and forty dollars to him it's worth it to us. We should keep it, Carl.'

'No, Wife, they don't figure that way in America. Men buy to sell. We buy for a home and a living; it's different. I'd meant to tell you that I talked to Baker. He told me about a new Swedish settlement near Red Wing, Minnesota — Vasa. He says we can homestead land out there not more than ten or fifteen miles from town. There's a church at Vasa and some day there will be a school.'

'A real school, Father? For us?' exclaimed Elna. Of course there were many good schools in Wisconsin, but in the Pine Lake region schools were conducted in English, and were at a great distance, too.

'A real school, Daughter. You children can get an education; you and Gus should be having it now. It's partly what we came to America for, and we mustn't miss the chance.'

The mother nodded approval. She was lucky to have a wise husband who planned well.

'Won't Gus be surprised!' giggled Elna. 'He doesn't know we have sold the place and are going to Minnesota — all in one day.'

'We've not finished either job yet, Daughter. And Gus may not be so pleased about leaving his good job. He'll be a long time finding friends like the smith and the kind coach driver.'

'Does Herr Lange give us a sled, Father?' asked Hans. 'He talked about a sled.'

'We have to make our own sled, Son. Come, we'll finish the chores now. Then this evening, when the boys are at home, we'll plan.'

Elna and Hans watched for Gustaf and when they saw him coming raced out to tell the news. He stared at them, unbelieving, till Elna repeated the tale.

'There's a school out at Vasa,' she added. 'That's one reason why we're going.'

'Oh, a school. You should tell that first, Sister. Though even for a school, I shall be sorry to leave my good job. But a school and a big farm — no wonder Father sells.'

That evening after supper, Gustaf brought in a great armful of firewood and the little cabin glowed with cheerful light. Elna set up a new sock; they would all need warm footwear for the long journey. The mother stood by the loom shifting the shuttle back and forth in quick rhythm. Hans carded wool by the hearth. Gustaf sharpened the axe on the wheel; Ernst and the father started making the sled. The beam on the plow the father was making would be set on the sled, handles and share would be packed.

'We'll take this table and the seats, Father?' Elna remarked. 'You made them so comfortable.' Her father studied the idea.

'The table, yes; the seats are but logs, upended. The table can be packed on the sled, upside down.'

'Suppose there is an early thaw and the sled won't pull?' asked Gustaf.

'Oh, Gus! Why suppose that?' His mother was dismayed.

'Better to suppose by the fire, comfortable,' said the father. 'Then we can plan. Now the snow is gone, Son. What then?'

'We might make two wheels, log sections, you know, Father. Speaking of the seats made me think. An iron for an axle; we could carry them on the sled. Then, come a thaw we could set the sled on wheels and go right along.' They studied the idea silently.

'We have a son with a good head, Mother,' said Larsson presently. 'Make us an axle at the smithy, Gus. We could saw wheels in a morning if we needed them. We'll take the axle along. Then, come snow, come thaw, we are ready.' Gustaf grinned. His father was pleased with the idea; it was good to use one's head and plan ahead.

Days, then weeks, went by. The sled, each part made by the fire in the evening, was now assembled in front of the cabin. The beam made of seasoned wood was fast ened firmly, the crossbar set so two could pull as with a plow. Work for the Bakers was finished, the pig butchered and salted down. Each person had new warm socks. The men's coats were mended; food enough for a fortnight was baked. Gustaf had fashioned the axle and three pieces of iron at the forge. Two pieces were shaped like a letter Y; the third was a bar to set across them, for hanging a kettle over the fire in camp.

But the weather stayed bitter cold — the coldest, so the smith claimed, for several years. This was no weather for starting out with a family and a cow.

On Tuesday, March 10, the sun shone and a gentle south wind blew warmly. Snow still crunched under foot, but the air promised spring.

'This is the day, Wife,' Larsson announced.

'We're going to Minnesota,' sang Hans. 'We are going to Minnesota today!' Waiting around ready, was tiresome business, he had learned. 'I'm walking all the way to Prairie du Chien and seeing Indians, too.'

Gustaf tweaked his ear. 'Save your Indians for Minnesota Territory. Haven't I told you there are none around here since the Black Hawk War twenty years ago? The smith told me.'

'But Herr Lange said ——'

'Herr Lange said many things that make trouble,' interrupted the mother tartly. Now that the moment of leaving was here, she was nearly sick with foreboding. 'Take this bundle and don't drop it in the snow, Elna. The Bible and Psalm Book are wrapped inside. Put it near the top,' she called to her husband. 'We shall need to read and pray for the good Lord's help.'

Anxiously the children hurried around; carry this,

78

hold that; fetch something else. The journey had seemed fun; now the mother's tense face made them fearful.

At last everything was packed. Blossom was watered and tied to the back of the sled. Gustaf stamped out the fire and looked around to make sure nothing was forgotten. Ernst fastened the door with a leather thong — and they were off.

Once away from the cabin spirits lifted. The sparkling sun, the gentle breeze stirred inherited love of adventure; walking on the hard snow was good. Perhaps everything would turn out for the best after all.

Hans and Elna raced the sled and hopped runners for a ride. The father and Gustaf, pulling, ran to evade them. The speed was too fast for Blossom.

'Here, I'll lead her,' suggested the mother. 'Then we'll see who can run the fastest.' She untied the rope and plodded along, leading the cow. Ernst took the father's place with Gustaf and the boys ran down the slope so fast that Elna and Hans had to give up.

'Mind you don't tip it over, boys!' Larsson shouted good-humoredly. 'Wait for us when you get to Prairie du Chien.'

Before noon they passed the end of the lake and Gustaf ran to bid the smith good-bye. The kind employer had been sorry to have Gustaf leave. He had offered to let him live at his own house; to raise his pay twenty-five cents a week; to give him a candle for evening study. But a fourteen-year-old boy had to go with his family. They needed him, too.

'Thought you'd be starting west this fine day,' he greeted Gustaf. 'I just said to Nelsen here, "Looks like spring. The Larssons will be starting." And here you are. But I'm sorry to see you go, Son. Luck to you!'

'Here's a bit for your journey, Gus.' Nelsen went inside the smithy and fetched a side of bacon, home-smoked, hanging from a string. 'It may taste good on the way. You did well with that latch and the hinges. You earned the bacon fairly.'

Gustaf flushed with pleasure. He had liked making the hardware for the Nelsens and had declined offered pay. But his mother would be pleased with the bacon and the idea that he had earned it. He accepted the gift gratefully.

'And here's something for your pocket,' said the smith, 'but don't get it wet.' He laid in Gustaf's hand a small pamphlet. 'I just got it from Madison. The coach driver brought it yesterday and a time we had keeping you from seeing it! Can you read it?' He looked eagerly at the boy's face.

Gustaf studied the title page. '"An Immigrants' Guide to Minnesota." Yes, I know those words. But I'll not be here to bring it back to him.'

'The book is yours, Gus. A right new one, it is! The driver got it from a man coming through from Prairie du Chien. He says it tells a person just what to do. Well, luck to you, Son.'

Gustaf shook the smith's hand hard till the man laughed and said, 'Anybody'd know you'd been working at a smithy, Son, a grip on you like that!'

Gustaf folded the book in his kerchief and put it into his inside pocket. Then, with a grateful good-bye to these two true friends, he ran to catch up with his family.

Mid-afternoon they reached Watertown. It was a

bit out of their way but the deal with Lange must be finished. Gustaf left the pastor's book at Swansson's house with a message to be given Pastor Hökansson in the spring. Larsson signed the final papers and got his money. He rolled it tightly in his money belt and buttoned his heavy fleece-lined coat over all.

'Take some lemon drops for the children,' Lange said. 'Take a handful. They'll need more food than you can carry, time you get to the river.'

Outside the town they stopped in a small grove. Larsson and Ernst gathered wood; Hans brought the iron rods for the pot and Gustaf pounded them deep into the snow. They held as firmly as though set in the ground in summer. Elna unpacked the pot, food, and bowls, Ernst got the fire going, Larsson fed and bedded Blossom. Soon the snow was melting in the pot and the porridge began bubbling. Blossom munched her fodder like a good traveler while the children scurried around unpacking bedding. The father read an evening psalm and they sang a favorite hymn before eating.

The night was cold. Hans and Elna were glad to crawl under the sled, where Gustaf made a bed for them by spreading a blanket on a hollow in the snow. Blossom lay at the side of the sled and her warmth made them comfortable.

For sixteen days the Larssons traveled, resting Sundays, making eight to twelve miles a day. Mostly the good weather held, though it was bitter cold at night and sometimes it seemed as though they had been walking forever.

On Thursday afternoon late in March they sighted the houses of the river town, Prairie du Chien and the great, wide Mississippi River.

81

'We'll camp here,' decided Larsson. 'We've no money for an inn.' Elna shivered with weariness and cold as they made camp. Gustaf ran ahead to explore.

'We're here!' he called back. 'I see the river! Ice is going out!' He watched the great floes, fascinated as they spun in the swift current. He did not dream that an ice floe was to make trouble for the Larsson family. He turned back cheerfully.

WAITING FOR THE BOAT

Chapter Eleven

'You stay here, Gus, and help your mother.' Carl Larsson folded his greatcoat around him to keep out that west wind. 'Ernst and I'll go to the town and look around. There's a lot of ice in the river. Not safe for a boat yet, I'd say.'

'We don't know this river, Carl,' Ernst remarked. 'The smith told Gus it's the longest river in the world. They didn't even find the beginning of it till twenty-five years ago. Maybe boats run different in this river.'

'Maybe' — Larsson was doubtful. 'We'll find out.' They set out down the bank.

Gustaf stood watching. He'd like to go with his father. His knowledge of English might be a help, though his skill was in reading, not talking. (There had been little chance for talk; only an occasional passenger on the bus.

Others he was with were Scandinavians.) But someone must stay with his mother. Hans wasn't old enough to fetch heavy wood, and near a town a person didn't feel as safe as out in the country.

From the high land he looked at the ice and snow piled along the river. Great boats crowded the landing, some of them shining and new. He didn't know till later that there were more boats carrying passengers and freight that year of 1857 than ever before. He saw some that had double decks and two great smokestacks. They looked large enough to carry hundreds. He walked back to their camp slowly.

'It's not going to thaw today,' his mother said. 'I'd thought I could wash.'

'Not this day, Mother. The west wind would freeze the water before you got a suds. I'll build a good fire to warm us. There's a lot of scrubwood around.'

'Could you make some soup, Mother?' asked Elna. 'Father said he'd be gone awhile.' Her teeth chattered and her nose was blue. Even the thought of hot soup was warming.

'That's a fine idea, Elna. We've a few potatoes left — I hope they're not frozen. I wrapped them with the blankets.' She unpacked bundles from the sled.

Soon the kettle was simmering and Elna huddled in the lee of Gustaf's good fire began to feel warmer. A good thing too, for when Larsson returned he reported that they must wait. There were plenty of boats, oh, yes.

'There are five new ones, built for this season. They're big and handsome ones. We can get passage all right, and not too costly, either. Trouble is, the weather.

WAITING FOR THE BOAT

Word came overland from Winona yesterday that the river is frozen solid there. The inns here are filled with people waiting to go upriver. We'll have to wait patiently till the ice goes out.' Strange news to travelers who had pushed hard each day lest they be late.

'Nice business!' Ernst was tired and disappointed. 'Sit on the snow and wait!'

Elna had a fit of coughing. Gustaf looked at her thoughtfully. She was still cold. He had a good fire, but the wind on that bluff was bitter.

'Let's build a snowhouse, Ernst,' he said.

'Not I! You and Hans can play childish games. I'm tired,' Ernst answered crossly.

'All right. Come on, Hans. First we get the snow.'

Along the crest, the snow lay in drifted hunks. Gustaf carried two, three, five and set them in a row west of the fire. Ernst looked on idly, not speaking. But when, soon, he saw a low wall shaping up, he realized Gustaf's plan. His ill humor vanished and he began to help. To keep off the worst of the wind they built a U-shaped shelter around the fire, and finished it off by laying long branches across for a roof that actually kept in some warmth and gave them all a feeling of protection.

Each morning Larsson went for news. Sometimes Gustaf went along, sometimes Ernst. The word brought back was always the same: no boat moving. They could see *that* from the bluff. The father tried to get work, but scores of men who filled the inns were trying that same thing and there was work for no one — Scandinavian, Swiss, Irish, or German. All were restless, eager to be gone. But the ice kept a tight grip on the river.

Days went by. Weeks. Idleness wearied them more

than work. Gustaf was thankful for his new book. He studied it frequently and read bits as best he could to his father. But weather was too cold to study or read long at a time; one must be moving. They were all hungry, too. The price of food in town was too high; Larsson knew he would need every penny to outfit his new home. So they pretended they had plenty as they drank hot melted snow flavored with a bit of corn or rye.

One morning Larsson came back early from the river-front. He was cold and tired and very discouraged.

'Did you buy anything, Father?' Hans asked hopefully. 'Mother is waiting to make dinner. We thought maybe ——' The look on his father's face answered Hans.

'We can make out, Son.' The father attempted to be cheerful. 'Everything is so costly in the village. Your mother can boil the rind of Nelsen's bacon. Lucky you got that, Gus. I never thought our own meat would go so quickly.'

'Walking in the cold makes us so hungry, Carl,' Ernst remarked.

'We've two nice bones, yet' — the mother stirred about cheerfully — 'and plenty of meal to thicken the stock and make it tasty. Hans, fetch me some wood; hurry and you won't feel the cold. I'll get the kettle on and you can smell dinner cooking.'

Gustaf walked back of the snowhouse and looked down at the village of Prairie du Chien spread before him. Somewhere down there, a person should be able to get food. The river, nearly half a mile away, was solidly white. Tall bluffs on the opposite side gleamed, their banks piled with ice and snow. A church spire sparkled in the morning sun. Houses of the village clustered around the boat landing and the church. Off to the south were the lowlands where the Wisconsin River, now ice-bound, too, would soon pour its waters into the Mississippi. Woods in the lowlands were dark with brush, blown clean of snow by the wind. A small black speck, a man, moved from the brush out onto the gleaming ice.

Instantly a thought came to Gustaf's mind. Stupid! Oaf! Why hadn't he thought of it before? Why hadn't any one of them? But, since they hadn't, he would make a surprise.

He walked back the few steps to the campfire, trying to be casual and not attract their attention. He needn't have worried. The Larssons were so cold and hungry they couldn't notice anything. Gustaf went into the snowhouse, rummaged among his things, put what he selected into his pocket and came out, wiping the cheerful grin off his face as he stood before his family.

'Mind if I walk along the river, Father?' he asked.

'No, Son. But you'll be cold. There isn't a thing doing. You can see from here that not a boat has made steam. No telling when they will, either.'

'I'll be no colder than sitting around here,' Gustaf replied mildly. 'Want to come along, Ernst?'

'Not I! Not a thing is doing in the whole town. Yesterday everyone was so tired and cross with the waiting that I'd rather stay here.'

'I'm just getting the bones on, so dinner will be later,' remarked the mother kindly. She scooped snow into the kettle and swung it over the fire. 'Take your time, Gus.'

He walked down the slope of the hill, along the trail

87

they had worn in the snow. The farther he got from camp, the more certain he felt that his idea was good, though he would feel better if he was sure it was allowed. And he would like company. Ernst wasn't a bit of fun these days. He walked briskly, then began to run. Better to go through the village first and see if he could find someone to question, then go through the bottom-lands.

Along the docks he eyed each person he passed; no one noticed him, and Gustaf hated to speak up boldly. Yet he really should know about the law. Just before he came to the Fur-Trading Post, he spied a boy, sitting on a great stone by the south wall. The lad had blond hair, blue eyes, strong shoulders, and a few freckles spread across his nose; he looked like a Swede. His hands were busy with stout twine as he tried to make the last loop of an intricate pattern. Gustaf watched a minute. Why, *he* knew that very trick!

'This is the way' — he spoke quickly, in Swedish, before he thought. 'Look! Put your thumb under, so. Now your third fingers, so. There. Now you have it!'

The boy looked from his fingers to Gustaf and grinned.

'I've been working for an hour to get that pattern. My uncle in Sweden used to trap rabbits with a snare like that. But he had to stop. It wasn't allowed.' He studied his string to make sure he had the pattern in mind. Then he looked at Gustaf.

'You're from Sweden.' It wasn't a question. They had used the language. 'Live here?'

'In Prairie du Chien? No. We camp on the bluff.' Gustaf nodded toward the bluffs in the east. 'We lived by Pine Lake, and now we go to Red Wing as soon as the ice goes out. Do you live here?'

'No, we came last night. From by Rockford. We go up the river, maybe to Winona. My father is a cabinet-maker. People tell him there is much work up the river.'

Gustaf looked at him with admiration, his own plans forgotten at the moment. To think he had spoken so boldly to a city boy! In Sweden a cabinet-maker in town would have thought himself much superior to a cotter's son.

'That's fine,' he said respectfully.

'I don't think it is,' the boy answered. 'Before we crossed the Wisconsin River we slid down a steep bluff and our cart turned over onto the ice. We had a bad time. All the tools spilled out. We found those, but Mother's plates were broken beyond mending and a tub of good food sunk in a hole in the ice. Father says it's the only thin place in the two rivers and of course he had to hit it.' The lad seemed glad to have a listener. 'I knew some boys in Rockford. And we had food. I thought maybe I could remember how to make a snare,' he added.

Gustaf sat beside him on the stone. The sun shone warmly on the south wall of the trading post; it was surprisingly comfortable there.

'Maybe there is a law about snaring,' he remarked.

'Oh, no!' The lad had no doubts. 'We've lived in Illinois two years now. Up here it's even more open. Snaring's all right — if you know how.'

'How about fishing?' Gustaf asked, remembering.

'Now, that's a good idea. Might be quicker than snaring. What's your name? Mine is Nels Lindholm.'

'Gustaf Larsson. Come on! I've a fishhook and line in my pocket. Let's go fishing.'

The two boys set off gaily, small discomforts like cold and hunger forgotten. Leaving the village, they skirted the hill where Fort Crawford stood guard, a reminder of Indian troubles, and plunged into the woods.

'There's a trail through here that meets the one we took yesterday. I think I can find it. Yes, here it is, Gus. Look! That's where our cart went last night. Down here we'll come to the Wisconsin River. Didn't you cross it?'

'Yes, but not here. Up the river the bluff wasn't so steep.' Gustaf looked up at the great bluff across the river. It would be hard, truly, to get a cart down that steep slope. 'Where are the fish, I wonder?'

'Round a water hole, waiting for us, I hope,' laughed Nels. 'We ought to catch suckers, at least. I got some through the ice last year down in Rock River. In summer I got trout and catfish. Anything would taste good to me today.'

'You were making a snare,' Gustaf remembered as they tramped along. 'What did you think you'd catch?'

'Muskrat, rabbits, beaver maybe. But my twine is too light. Fish are a better chance since you have line and hook.'

'Look!' Gustaf stopped suddenly. 'Those are rabbit tracks. Let's set your snare here, just in case.'

Nels handed over the twine and Gustaf's fingers quickly made it into a tight pattern. This he set under a bush just over the prints of tiny feet.

'You make a good snare,' said Nels.

'My grandfather Anders taught me. You're right, the

twine is not strong. But it might hold; worth a try.'
Nels shook snow from an overhanging branch to blot out
most of their footprints. 'We're more likely to get fish.'

Not far from the bank they found a hole, a promising
place. Gustaf took line and hook from his pocket,
shaved a thin curl of bacon rind, and fastened it firmly
to the hook. They squatted Eskimo fashion by the hole,
and Gustaf let down the line. There was much they
would like to talk of, but they waited silently.

The line jerked. Gustaf tensed his arms, let the fish
take hold, and landed it neatly. Nels sprang to take it
from the hook.

'He didn't even take the bait!' he gloated. 'Where'll
I put him, Gus?'

'I've a line to string him on.' Gustaf pulled it from his
pocket. 'I wondered if I was too hopeful when I brought
it.' In a jiffy Nels had the fish strung on, a stick tied at
the end, and the fish laid in a snowbank.

'That's yours, Nels, because you knew of this good
place.'

'Silly! It's your idea and your line.'

'Maybe we'll catch more.'

To their amazement, they got ten, but by that time
the sun was nearly set and their feet were icy lumps
that ached.

'That's enough for this day. We'll come again tomorrow,' Gustaf decided. They divided the catch
fairly. The snare was empty, but that could wait another day.

Gustaf was eager to get home. Fresh broiled fish
would taste wonderfully good. His mouth watered as he
ran. How stupid not to have thought of fishing before!

Blood came back into his cramped legs, but his fingers and feet stayed numb till he rubbed them with snow by the fire.

The surprise was even better than he expected. Each person had a half a fish; the rest was divided evenly. Nor was that the last. Nels and Gustaf fished each day. Luck wasn't always as good as at first; once it was better — his mother had six fish left over, which she buried in the snow. They caught nothing in the snare. Gustaf didn't know why.

'Before we leave, Father,' he planned, 'I'm going to catch a lot of fish. Mother can cook them and they'll be good eating on the boat. We needn't be hungry again. But I wish Nels was going to Red Wing.'

Chapter Twelve

ON A Wednesday, the third week in April, **Larsson** came
back from the village on a run.

'The *Galena's* going to start this afternoon. Look!
She's making up steam now.' He pointed west; they saw

93

puffs of smoke rising from one of the boats. 'She's not one of the newest boats. The captain — his name is Laughton — says he's not afraid to butt the ice. He wants to be first up the river. Gets him higher prices for his load if he's the first.' Larsson had no trouble, now, picking up news. He understood English better than he could speak it. He had learned to say, 'Yag, I speaka Anglish,' and this encouraged people to talk to him. Then, too, there were several Swedish men in the village who, like Lindholm, were waiting to go to towns up the river. Some of them had been in the United States long enough to speak English very well. They were friendly and talked over news they gathered.

'Come. We must hurry to pack and get aboard.' The mother could hardly wait to be off.

'Not on the first boat, Wife. That costs extra. Two boats plan to leave tomorrow. We'll try for one of those. People say, "Get your family and your goods down by the landing. Then make your bargain. No captain wants to take a cow. But if you are there, ready, you stand a better chance."'

'What boats go tomorrow, Father?' asked Elna. Her cold was better now. She was rested from the long walk. That hurried trip had been hard for Elna and Hans.

'Well, there's an old boat, the *War Eagle*. We should try for her on account of Blossom. The *Northern Light* is going. She was new last year. You can see her white paint from here. She was built somewhere up the Ohio River; most of the boats were, I'm told. We'll have a look at her tomorrow.'

When Gustaf came back with his fish, late in the afternoon, they ran to tell him the news.

'Go tomorrow? Fine! But today I got the smallest catch yet. I'll be up early and do better tomorrow, maybe.'

'Fish are nice, Gus, but tomorrow you are to stay right here with us,' commanded his mother. 'With your father doing this, so sudden-like after all the waiting, would you risk being left behind? Fish are good, but to keep together is better.'

Larsson nodded.

'Maybe I could run now and tell Nels that we leave,' said Gustaf.

'Go back to the village *now?*' The father's voice was disapproving. 'Better to risk the chance of seeing him tomorrow, Gus, than to wear yourself out walking back and forth. We have work to do tomorrow.'

Gustaf gazed at the flames thoughtfully as he warmed himself by the campfire after supper. Nels seemed a good friend; yet he had known him but six days. If they got a place on a boat tomorrow he might never see Nels again. At least he could watch carefully in the village and tell Nels good-bye.

The Larssons were up at dawn. Breakfast over, they packed the sled snugly and started down the bluff. The sun was shining brilliantly. Surely the ice would let them go now.

Larsson hurried from one boat to the next, learning about prices, freight, and departures. Gustaf stood by the sled, but he scanned every face in sight, hoping Nels would happen by. Not a person Gustaf had ever seen passed.

The handsome *Northern Light* was finally loaded but Captain Lodwick lingered. He had a little more space on the lower deck; empty space was money out of pocket on the first trip of his season. He saw Larsson.

'Hey, you!' he shouted. 'Going upriver?'

'Yag! Red Wing!' Larsson answered.

'Family?' The captain hesitated before giving the order to cast off.

'Six!' Larsson held up his hand to show the number. 'And a cow.'

'He *would* have a cow!' The captain swore loudly.

'Well, get a move on! I'll take the lot of you for ten dollars. Put your cow near the rail by the lower deck and keep her well bedded. Move, now, Swede!'

Luckily Carl Larsson was a fast runner and had had training in the races he ran in Sweden. He had need of speed now. He dashed up the road by the landing where he had left his family with the sled.

'Anna Marie! Elna, Hans! Take the bundles and get aboard the boat.'

'Not one step will I go till you are with us, Carl,' said the mother fearfully.

'Stop such chatter and get aboard to save the place. The captain will not cast off till I come; *I*, with the passage money.'

'Stupid that I am. Children! Come quickly! Gus, take this bundle.'

'Gus helps with the sled, Wife. You lead Blossom. We mustn't keep them waiting.'

Hans picked up the nearly empty bread sack Elna shouldered a bundle and helped to coax Blossom. The cow liked neither the crowd nor the gangplank, when she came to it. The father, Ernst, and Gustaf picked up the loaded sled, carried it along the levee, and dragged it aboard. Smoke poured in dark clouds from the twin stacks; the captain shouted the order to cast off. While the Larssons held the timid Blossom, the great boat moved away from the shore. Gustaf watched for Nels until the people blurred in the distance.

'Maybe he's waiting for me at the fishing hole,' he thought. 'I'd have liked to tell him good-bye. He was a good friend.'

In summer, the weather warm, shoreline green, it would have been a fine trip. The tiny villages, squatters' huts, and wooded islands would have made interesting sights. But this day, the wind had turned cold again, the riverbanks looked dreary; the boat was packed with restless people talking loudly words the Larssons did not understand. They huddled together on the lower deck. Never since the crowds and noises of Castle Garden in New York had they been a part of such confusion. They looked silently at each other, longing for the peace of the Pine Lake home. Once it had seemed fine to have so much money. Now they were sorry they had sold the cabin. They had been so happy there.

Blossom hated the boat. She stamped and protested. Gustaf tossed a blanket over her head, covering her eyes; he patted and talked with her for some time before she finally settled down.

All afternoon, all night, the side paddles turned steadily. Stops were made for wood, stacked ready at landings along the way. On the upper deck were a few stylish staterooms, all occupied, of course. Many passengers, like the Larssons, had no money to pay for comfort. Others, able to pay, preferred to crowd onto this boat rather than to wait longer at Prairie du Chien. Every

inch of floor was taken and people milled around rest-
lessly. No one slept much. The boat moved slowly,
battling the ice and the strong current.

When they reached the south end of Lake Pepin they
found the *Galena*, the *Itasca*, and a score of smaller boats
held up by the ice.

'I'll bet it's May afore I get to St. Paul!' complained
Captain Laughton.

'The *Lady Franklin* got there the middle of April last
year,' Captain Lodwick shouted across as the boats
rubbed together. 'First boat up' was an honor each captain tried to win and was always remembered. 'Such
ice! It'll be morning before we start up the lake, I'll be
bound.'

Bold men and boys jumped from the boat onto the ice
floes, great broad sheets of ice that looked solid as land
and bumped noisily into the *Northern Light*. Gustaf
wished to join this fun, but Blossom set up such a bellow-
ing he couldn't leave her. The rhythmic churn of the
paddles had stopped. Instead, ice bumped and jarred the
boat.

'I'll draw some water for her, Mother,' Gustaf said.
'I'll be right back.'

Picking up the bucket, he went to the opening by
the gangplank, threw his arm around a post, and
dipped down into the lake. Just then a great floe hit
the boat with a whack and threw him back onto the
deck.

That crash was too much for Blossom. With a mighty
yank of her head, she broke her rope, pushed Mrs. Larsson aside, made for the opening, and plunged out onto
an ice floe. It tipped with her sudden weight. Slowly,

98

steadily, right before their eyes, Blossom slid into the icy water.

'Look! The Swede has lost his cow!' shouted a voice from the upper deck. Passengers ran to see. The boat listed dangerously.

'Back to the middle!' the captain yelled. 'Back, I say! You'll drown us all. Haven't you ever seen a cow before? Get back to the middle!' Shouting, swearing, he drove the passengers back from the rail. The *Northern Light* righted; was safe.

But Blossom was gone.

'Bet they don't even get her hide for shoes,' remarked someone.

'Whose was it?' asked another.

'Belonged to that Swede on the lower deck,' the captain said. 'He's taking his family to Red Wing.'

'Joke on him to lose his cow.'

But it was no joke to the Larssons. Blossom was a friend and an investment; more important still, she was a provider. Without her warm milk they would be hungrier than ever.

Gustaf felt a great emptiness below his ribs. But there was nothing to do but tighten his belt and hope to reach Red Wing soon.

Chapter Thirteen

THE minute the *Northern Light* touched the wharf at
Red Wing, Carl Larsson jumped ashore and ran up the
street to the land agent's office. Lange had said that land
the United States Government had bought from the
Dakota Indians five years before was the best farm land

100

in the world. Larsson meant to homestead on that. He had planned exactly what to do. In the cabin at Pine Lake while he worked on the sled, he had repeated Lange's words over and over. Huddled over the campfire in the evenings as they journeyed across Wisconsin, Gustaf had read from the 'Immigrants' Guide' the smith had given him and translated all he understood for his father. Larsson had pieced together every bit he knew about taking up a claim, and now as he hurried up the street he said it over like a lesson.

'Get to the land agent's office *first*. Swear out your intention to become a citizen of the United States. Insist on getting surveyed land.' (The title might some day be disputed if the land wasn't properly surveyed.) 'File your papers and make sure they are correct. Get a Swede to help you there in Red Wing, if you can find one' — this was Lange's idea. 'But the agent there — W. W. Phelps is his name — is an honest man. You'll have no trouble if you're careful.' And Larsson meant to use every care. This time, he intended to settle permanently. Minnesota, the land of sky-blue waters, was to be his home.

Gustaf and Ernst, left behind, dragged the sled from the boat, put it in a sheltered corner, and piled the bundles upon it. Now they could watch the crowds. The *Northern Light* was the second boat in; the *Galena* had stopped only an hour because Captain Laughton was determined to be the first into Saint Paul. (He made it, too; but Gustaf didn't know that until years afterward, when he happened to read it in a book.) People from the town came down to watch the unloading. Merchants bid high for goods.

101

'Boy! You, boys! Can't you lend us a hand?' someone called. The man rubbed his long whiskers nervously as he came near Gustaf and Ernst, guarding their possessions. 'I can't get a man for love or wages and the captain says I have to move my stuff at once.'

The two boys hesitated, uncertain whether they understood.

'Give you half a dollar for the rest of the day if you're strong as you look and will hustle.' Gustaf tossed his heavy coat to Elna, buttoned his blue jacket, and followed the man. Ernst was close behind him. Elna, Hans, and the mother watched as the boys staggered under great boxes and barrels they carried from the boat. Gustaf called to them gaily.

'Anyone here who can cook?' shouted another worried man. The Swiss hotelkeeper went up and down the landing shouting his woe. 'Got my hotel full of people and my cook engages on the *Galena*. Never even tells me she's going! Any cook here?'

People laughed. No one volunteered. A third boat was coming up the river. Another person's trouble wasn't interesting.

'Say! Boy! That your mother over there? Can she cook?'

Gus hesitated. Was the man speaking to him? Could his mother cook? Of course! Any Swedish woman could cook. His mother was one of the best. Silly question. He lifted a heavy bale of goods to his shoulder.

The Swiss waited for him. 'That's your mother, Son. I saw you speak to her. She doesn't understand me. If she can cook, I'll give her a job and you can all sleep over the barn. I've a hotel full of guests this minute and

102

not a woman around who can cook.' Now that the man spoke quietly Gustaf could understand. If people would only speak slowly and quietly instead of shouting, he understood English words fairly well. He went to his mother.

'He wants you to cook at his hotel, Mother. I can't leave, but if you want to go and see about it, I'll watch the children.'

'No one needs to watch us!' said Elna with spirit. 'We're not babies. We'll stay right here till Father comes.' She sat down by the bundles determinedly, watching the moving crowds. The mother hurried off behind the hotelkeeper.

Many men and boys jostled each other on and off the gangplank carrying the great loads. Gus had hardly set down a bale when two bearers bumped together and knocked a great box from the tall one's shoulders. For a second it balanced precariously on the edge of the plank, then dropped into the river.

'Here, you! Get that box out of the water! It's full of books!' A handsomely dressed, bewhiskered gentleman hurried from the top deck, dignity forgotten as he scolded the careless men.

'That's Judge Eli Turner from Ohio,' said an onlooker. 'He's come to open an office in Red Wing. We need a good lawyer here, for a fact.'

'Someone get those books out of the water!' the judge was shouting as he hurried down to the lower deck. At the word 'books,' Gus rushed to the gangplank. The water wasn't deep there; he could see the box. He swung himself down into the water. Getting a good grip on the box with both hands, he lifted it to the gangplank, where

103

the owner steadied it while Gustaf floundered up the bank. Getting out of the river was harder than jumping in.

'I'll get a crowbar, sir!' Dripping as he was, Gustaf ran to his bundle, got a small, sharp crowbar, and opened the box.

'You're a smart boy, Son.' The judge was much relieved. 'Not everyone would know that a box of wet books must be opened at once.'

Gustaf grinned happily and shoved his hair from his eyes. How lucky he was to have the chance to help a man like this! He pried off the box lid and tenderly lifted out the handsome calf-bound books. They were hardly damp. Wipe them with a cloth and they would be good as new. The paper lining in the box and his quickness had saved them. The judge stood by watching as Gustaf wiped each volume with a bit of linen from his mother's bundle, and piled them neatly in the sunshine.

'Take those damp papers out, Son, fold this dry one for the bottom and the books can go back in the box long enough to carry them uptown. Here, you stay by them while I get my valise from the boat. I've got to get me a room somewhere, quickly.' A few minutes later, Gustaf shouldered the books and followed the judge to the hotel where he set them down in the office, suddenly realizing that he should hurry back to his job. He was pleased with the great silver dollar the judge paid him, but even more pleased to know the judge was there.

'See you again, Son,' the judge had said. . . . 'See you again!' The words were like music.

Carl Larsson didn't return for six hours. He hadn't dared leave till he had his papers.

'Now, then,' he said to Elna and Hans, 'we'll call the

104

boys and get started. It's only about thirty miles, the agent says, and good going until a thaw. Where's your mother? Where's Gus? And Ernst?' He looked around blankly, suddenly missing them.

'They've jobs,' said Elna, nearly bursting with eager-ness to tell the news. 'Gus and Ernst got theirs first, fifty-cent ones, and Mother's the cook at the hotel.'

Her father laid his hand on her forehead tenderly. Was the child sick? Or had she gone daft with all the excitement?

Elna's happy giggle relieved him. 'She's at the hotel, Father, really. I'm fine.'

'What hotel? Where?'

'The tall building.' She pointed up the street. 'It's real pretty, isn't it? We're to sleep in the loft over the barn in back of it. Gus knows about it and you needn't worry.'

But Larsson hadn't waited to hear more. He ran like mad up the street to the building marked *Red Wing Hotel*. Yes, Anna Marie was in the kitchen, pleased as Punch to be working with good food; plenty of flour — wheat, rye, and buckwheat. Plenty! Imagine that! And corn meal, butter, eggs, and sugar just brought from the boat. Fragrant smells wafted from the stove; the hotelkeeper greeted Larsson with cordial words — not one of which was understood.

'Bring your family to supper! Stay here! Stay all summer!' Already he knew his good luck in getting such a cook.

Anna Marie smiled at her husband. 'Bring the chil-dren over, Carl, and put our things in the shed. I'm making bread — you'll never believe the sour stuff these

105

people have been eating. Guests come soon, he says, so I cannot leave to talk. Carl' — she motioned for him to come close as she kneaded the bread — 'he calls me "Mrs. Larsson" — as though I was a lady! That's America for you!'

That night in the loft new plans were made. Larsson would go alone to stake his claim; he could make good time without a load. The boys could work at the landing. Pay was good even though the work was heavy. The mother would cook for the wages of three dollars a week. Who ever heard of such big pay? And board for Elna and Hans and herself, too. Gus and Ernst could sleep in the loft, free. Meals would cost them twenty-five cents a day. Such good luck made them forget to mourn for Blossom.

The next morning Larsson left for the West. He was gone three weeks; weeks during which immigrants arrived in Red Wing daily. The town was crowded. Stores displayed merchandise from St. Louis and even from New York, for now the railroad carried Eastern freight to Galena, where it was loaded onto boats for river towns. Gustaf and Ernst worked every day and had offers of jobs at the sawmill, started two years before, if they wished to change from unloading.

Elna learned to help at the hotel and to run errands for travelers. Hans fed the chickens and waited on his mother. Sometimes they went to watch boats. The tall stacks belched black smoke in handsome patterns; the paddles turned in smooth rhythms, enchanting to hear. The boats looked like swans, Hans thought, all but the smoke, as they turned out or in, near the landing.

Larsson came back to town full of enthusiasm. 'It's a

grand country! And we have fine land. I stepped off the whole one hundred and sixty acres. We plow a furrow all around it as soon as we get out there.'

'One hundred and sixty acres!' The mother had never quite believed. 'That's enough for six families.'

'We'll need it!' The father laughed at her amazement. 'Ernst can't get land for himself until he's twenty-one. By then, good land near us may be gone. Gus will want some, too.'

'I'd rather live in town when I'm grown,' said Gustaf. 'I've decided to be a lawyer. Judge Turner says they'll need good lawyers out here.'

Larsson looked at his son, surprised. The boy surely had developed. 'I'd be proud to have you a lawyer, Son. But you'd want land just the same.'

'I'll want land,' spoke up Hans. 'I'll not live in town. I want to farm.'

'Good for you, Hans! Every man to his taste. Now, come morning, we'll rent an oxteam to haul our things and plow some land. Ernst can drive it back to town.

'I'll buy a big strong plow. That small plow I made at the smithy will do us for the garden plot, but we need a big plow to break ground for the main crop. We can't worry with a small plow when we tackle that tough prairie grass in a big field. You should see the stuff! Then I'll buy tools and some things for our house. Maybe you'd like a cookstove, Anna Marie.'

'Listen to my man,' laughed the mother. 'We shall buy tools we must have, and food, but the rest of our money we pay on the land. Or do they *give* land to a man like you?'

'Not give, though it is in a way a gift, for it is so cheap,

Land costs a dollar and twenty-five cents an acre; beautiful land. And we have twenty years to pay.'

'All the same, I do not like debt. Not even twenty years of debt.' The mother was firm. 'We buy what we must. The rest is for the land. It will be ours the sooner. Now to sleep all of you or we shall not be ready for to-morrow.'

Elna turned toward the wall and shut her eyes. But it was hard to settle down when so much was in her mind. A new home, one hundred and sixty acres. Why, a *dozen* farms in Sweden would not be that big, not all together. They would have a real house some day; her mother spoke of it often. The town of Vasa was near their farm. Vasa. It had a nice sound as she whispered it. Her father liked the village; said it was started by a Swede, Hans Mattson, four years ago. There was a church there; maybe a school. Perhaps she could learn to read a book and have nice ways and be like Mrs. Baker.

'Perhaps some day Father will have sheep and I can have some tallow to make that nice lotion Mrs. Baker uses to keep her hands soft.' Mrs. Bergvaal had given Elna the recipe; it was tucked in her pocket right now. Tallow and verbena or geranium leaves, it called for. And perhaps some day Elna could have a dress from St. Louis. Likely that was just a dream.

As Mrs. Larsson tucked the blanket around Hans, she thought of the woman who was taking her place at the hotel, a strong, cheerful person, cousin of the storekeeper who had recently come up from St. Louis. 'I must tell her to set the bread early each evening and put the bowl on a stool near the oven. It rises better when it gets a start before the oven cools. She'll like cooking with such good food as they have here.' Then her thoughts turned to the next day's journey and she planned the food she must make ready.

Gustaf, rolled in his blanket across the room, had his thoughts, too. This spring and summer he would work for his father, of course. But perhaps by fall he could come to town and stay during the winter. Judge Turner had rented two rooms over a store. Gustaf had helped him unpack and arrange his books. The judge planned to take his meals at the hotel but he would be glad to have some one to tend his fires and do chores; he had half-promised to keep the place for Gustaf.

'In the morning I'll go around and tell him we leave for the farm,' Gustaf said to himself. He made up sentences in English and rehearsed exactly what he wished to say. The judge had told him that a lawyer who knew English *and* Swedish could get a lot of business in this new country. So many immigrants were coming out to homestead now, and few could speak English. Gustaf fell asleep, counting weeks until fall.

THE SOD HOUSE

Chapter Fourteen

THE day was beautiful, warm with late May sunshine, tempered with a gentle breeze. The children were glad to leave the bustle of Red Wing and to have freedom to run and play. Wild flowers bloomed in profusion. The land rolled west; no hills, only a smooth roll like an ocean on a good day. The sturdy rented oxen plodded along, making about two miles an hour. They didn't mind the heavy load and needed only an occasional prod or a shouted 'Gee!' or 'Haw!' to keep them on their way.

Larsson had made many purchases. He bought the heavy new-styled plow, made in Illinois, as he had planned; a cookstove, two kettles, a tub, a small door and window for the new house, a keg of nails, a saw. He also had seed potatoes, wheat and a small amount of rye and barley seed for planting. All these new things, together with the sled carefully taken apart and the Wisconsin things, were loaded on the rented cart.

'We wrote a letter to Grandfather and Grandmother while you were away, Father.' Elna stopped her play to walk by her father for a while. 'Mother bought the stamp. The letter went on the *Itasca* to Galena and a train carries it to New York. The captain says it will get there in two months.'

'Mother wrote the letter,' Gustaf added, coming near. 'But the paper was light and thin, so we could all write at the end and still need but one stamp.'

'You told them about the new land?'

'Oh, yes, Father! Though they will hardly believe you have one hundred and sixty acres all your own!'

'It *will* be our own, remember, Son. It's only half paid for now, but we'll hope to have it all ours by another summer. We shall work hard, Gus.' Gustaf nodded. He understood the responsibility his father had taken on.

'Living is better here than in Wisconsin, Father,' he remarked after a while. 'The Swiss says there is a lot of game around. And Indians are friendly. They bring in venison so there is plenty of meat without killing stock. Game's easy to catch, he says. He showed me how to make a snare for muskrat. I see now how Nels and I had it wrong. No wonder we didn't catch anything. Mother cooks them to taste like chicken.'

'We'll hunt after the crop is in, Gus. Wheat and barley go in first. Then flax. There's not such a hurry about corn and potatoes. Once the crop's in we can take it easier. The soil's worth work.' Gustaf and Ernst looked at the earth as Larsson kicked a bare hillock.

'See how good it is, boys? Fine black loam. And clay underneath to make it drain well.' He was so happy he started singing gaily, loudly. They all joined in and sang themselves breathless.

'Is there a cabin here, Father?' Gustaf asked after a while. 'There was at Pine Lake.'

'Aye, because Pearman built it. No one has lived on Minnesota land except Indians, and they don't build cabins. We'll build our own shelter.'

'Can we build a cabin with a loft, Father?' Gustaf had been thinking about this. In a loft, he could study by candlelight, evenings, away from the distracting family talk. 'It wouldn't be much more work and Ernst and I could sleep there. I'd make the ladder.'

His father frowned worriedly. His family might not like his decision on this.

'We have no time to cut logs and build a cabin now. Got to get the crop in and the team back to town.' They stared at him, amazed.

'Where shall we live, Father?' Hans asked. 'We always have a home.'

'We shall now, Hans. Made of sod instead of logs.'

'Of *sod!* Sod is dirt!' The mother stepped nearer to hear his answer. She had heard people in Red Wing speak of sod houses but had thought nothing of it. *Her* husband was a good builder; *they* would have a house of logs. 'A sod house would wash out with the rain.'

'Wash out!' teased Ernst. 'Ask Elna about that!'

Elna flushed and made a face at him. 'Gus fixed it better than before. Anyway ——'

'But tell us, Carl,' the mother interrupted.

112

THE SOD HOUSE

'It's only for a while, Wife. Feel this thick prairie grass? Cut in blocks, it makes a good house — warm in winter; cool in summer. We've a stove for cooking and a real window with glass; a door with a latch. I bought sailcloth for the ceiling so the dirt won't drop on us. Some don't spend for that. You'll see sod houses soon now. Come winter, we'll fell logs and you shall have a good house, bigger than Pearman's. You'll see.'

The going was easy now except when they came to a thorn thicket or low-lying swamp grass and had to go around. At noon the next day they came to Vasa, the Swedish town. In Red Wing most people talked English or German or Norwegian; here, all talk was Swedish. People gathered around and called them neighbors; made them welcome. Doubts Mrs. Larsson had about the sod house seemed suddenly petty. They'd manage; they always had. The children were thrilled to see other children with whom they could talk.

Pastor Norelius was away on the missionary trip, northwest; but his wife invited them to the parsonage, a tiny cabin, eight feet square, sunshine glinting through the slimsy roof. They shared the dinner she was cooking and heard about the church and school.

'The church was organized a year and a half ago,' she said as she dished up the dinner. 'Carl Carlsson — he stands out there talking to your husband now — had the first meeting in his cabin. Later we built the church; it's big, sixteen square, good logs. Sit here, children. Gus can take his bowl out and talk to the big boys. Eat all you want.'

It seemed like coming home after a long journey. Later, when they left, people wished them luck.

'We'll be over in about a week and help roof your house,' Carlsson called.

'But it's a busy time,' Larsson answered. 'I don't want to bother you.'

'Don't fret yourself. We've time to help a neighbor.' He made sure where the claim was. 'Have the boys cut the sod and make the walls. We'll roof it in no time.'

The children asked a dozen questions as they walked on, west. How was sod cut? When could they go to school? Would they get a cow? Or sheep? Or pigs?

The sun made long shadows by the time they came to a place where the land sloped gently southward to a creek. The grove on higher land had oak, maple, and elm trees, their dainty hints of new green a pretty color. To the east, two hickory nut trees and a few butternuts were still bare of leaf. To the west wild plum and cherry trees were white with bloom. Further on, a clump of hazelnut bushes grew near a widened bit of the creek, almost like a tiny lake. Beyond, a swampy meadow was green with grass, fine for fodder.

White and purple pasque-flowers lined the border of the creek, violets and fringed gentians near the plum trees made colorful shadows. A few minutes earlier they had passed the stake at the edge of his claim, but Larsson had not spoken; he wanted a surprise. He stopped, now, and pointed south.

'This is home.'

'Here? Oh, Father!' Gustaf, none of them, could say another word. The oxen were glad to pause. They switched their tails patiently and eyed the water in the creek.

Not in Wisconsin, not along the Mississippi, not since

114

THE SOD HOUSE

they left Red Wing, had the Larssons seen a more beautiful spot. On all sides the land rolled, flat enough for easy plowing; rolling enough for good drainage. Wood, aplenty, grew in the groves; water was right at hand; thick woods to the west promised game. The Larssons had come home.

'Shall we build the sod house here, Father?' Gustaf stood on the perfect site for a house: near the creek, high enough for a view.

'I've marked that in my mind for the log house, Son,' his father answered. 'You're right, it's a good place. They tell me, "Don't put your sod house where you want your house later." We'll build the sod home there, up higher. Gives more slope. A sod house cuts into the hill for one wall, you know. Then, when we have the cabin, the sod house will be back there for a storage house or for cattle.'

'May I begin cutting sod now, Father?' Gus tossed his blue coat aside, ready.

'Tonight? Not so fast, Gus. Make a fire for your mother and set the crane. Gather wood for tomorrow and unpack tools. After supper maybe we can mark a line and I'll show you how to cut sod. Use the spade first, Carlsson said, then loosen it with the grub-hoe. You can work between times of helping your mother. Ernst and I will plow. The team has to be back in Red Wing in a fortnight; I want to plow five acres and run a furrow all around. The agent said to get that in, for other settlers will be coming.'

Gustaf unloaded the fire rack and pot. 'I can't hurry the settling,' he thought to himself. Chores every day would take so much time that special work would go slowly. He'd have to forget about the judge and getting back to town until fall. It was right for a boy to stay and help his family.

He laid small sticks and rubbed a spark to flame. Hans carried the kettle to the creek; Ernst unyoked the oxen; Elna fetched the bread sack from the cart and unpacked bowls and spoons. Larsson unloaded bundles and his wife measured food. All worked willingly, happily. This was home.

Chapter Fifteen

'IT IS a good thing you got the big plow and the oxen,
Father,' said Gustaf. He wiped sweat from his forehead
as they paused at the end of a row. 'This tough prairie
grass would be hard to break with a hand plow.'

Larsson looked back over the way they had come. Not
more than half the field he had marked was turned, and
this was afternoon of the second day's plowing. Strong
as he was, Larsson's muscles ached more than he would
admit; to hold the plow steady and straight taxed even
his strength.

'You're right. It is slow, hard work. But it will never

take so long again, Son. Next year we'll start early and these fields we plow this year will be easy. Each year we'll turn some new.' He looked across his land proudly. Even hard work seemed agreeable when he remembered that this wonderful land was his own.

'The clods are big, Father,' Gustaf remarked as he gathered up the reins he had let go slack. 'Shall we plow it again?'

'If we have time with the team, we shall. If we don't I'll do what Swansson told me he did. We'll cut down a tree — we'll need some down anyway — and drag the whole tree-top over the field. He says it harrows and smooths the best way; with one pulling, too. Well, here goes, Gus.' He grasped the handles of the plow firmly. Gustaf tightened the reins and shouted to the oxen. Slowly they plodded across the field.

Ernst had driven the oxen all morning while Gustaf cut sod blocks and began digging in the side of the hill for one wall of the new house. Larsson had soon realized that it was better to have the boys, Ernst and Gustaf, alternate with chores or sod cutting and driving the oxen. So Ernst worked in the fields mornings and Gustaf in the afternoons. Larsson himself worked at the plow ten to twelve hours a day, and would have to keep up that rate if he was to get all the work he hoped from the oxen before they went back to Red Wing in a fortnight as promised.

Setting the sod blocks for the house was no easy matter either. If the house was to be ready for roofing by the time the men came over from Vasa, the boys would have to keep at the job more steadily than Larsson at first realized.

BIG WHISTLE

The sun shone warmly. A gentle breeze from the southwest sprang up, cool and dry.

'Look at that gopher run!' Gustaf laughed gaily. 'We must have hit another hole, Father. This field is full of them. Are they good to eat?'

'Not that I ever heard of. They're pretty little creatures, though. Soon as we get the crop in and the house finished, you and I are going hunting, Gus. No one need go hungry for meat out here. Swansson says there's plenty of game. But I never heard of eating gophers. I don't aim to start it.'

A flock of blackbirds passed overhead and settled on a thorn thicket at the south. 'Now, some of those would be good eating. They'd make a fine pie. Blackbirds might be a pest, come harvest, too, if they nest around here. . . . Well, now, is that more limestone? Lucky we don't come on it often.' He steadied the plow as it turned up a fairly large, thin stone. He lifted it away from the plow, brushed off the dirt and admired it.

'That's a pretty one, Gus. Mother will like it for a doorstone. I'll carry it home for her when we go.'

The sun was near the horizon before Larsson finally said, 'Well, Son, if we're to get the oxen watered and fed before dark, we'll have to stop work now. The plow can stay right here tonight; the sky is clear.' He unhooked the oxen and Gustaf started them toward home.

For an hour Gustaf had been watching supper preparations on the slope near where the sod house was being built. But each time they neared the creek, Larsson had turned away to plow another row, and still another. Now, Gustaf let the oxen drink at the creek and he washed his face and hands, ducking his hot head

119

under the water. How clean and fresh and cool it felt!

'Here, you!' he reproved the oxen. 'You can't drink more. Enough's enough! If you drink your fill you'll have no room for supper.' He pulled them away, drove them up the slope, and tied them to a tree. 'Now you shall have some good prairie grass I cut yesterday.' They eyed him, liking his quiet voice. He tossed before them armfuls of grass, the fresh green of new growth mixed with matted straw and seed heads of last year's. It made fine fodder. Gustaf ran back to the campfire, where porridge bubbled in the pot. Even on a warm night, hot porridge tasted fine after a day's hard work.

'Before you start on the sod cutting,' remarked Larsson as they finished eating, 'you'd better get your mother some more firewood, Gus. Ernst and I shall build up the blocks we have cut. You go over to the grove, east there. By that clump of trees you'll find a lot of windfalls and scrubwood. Fetch plenty while you're at it and you won't have to stop again for a few days. Hans, you go with Gus and carry all you can. Stack it near, so your mother can get at it handy.'

Hans was glad to go. He had very little time with Gustaf now. He felt important to be sent to help.

'Wait a minute, I'll get a board,' Gustaf said. 'I've a piece of rope in my pocket. I think I can make a drag. We'll load heavy sticks on my board and drag them home. This grass is so slick dragging ought to be easier than carrying. We'll try it.' He took one of the boards that had made the sled, tucked it under his arm, and they set out.

BIG WHISTLE

The clump of trees his father had pointed out was near a bend in the creek, half-hidden from the campfire by the slope; it was shadowy in the twilight. Gustaf leaned the board against a tree and began hunting wood. Great branches had been blown down by winter storms; some were dry and brittle, easy to break; some, not so dry, he laid aside till later. The driest would make quick fires; his mother would like that.

Both boys worked steadily. Time for talk after the light faded. Suddenly Gustaf looked up, and rubbed his eyes in amazement. What was *that?* A *man?* He made no movement; yet Gustaf would have sworn he wasn't there a minute ago.

The tall figure leaned against a tree carelessly, watching Gustaf. Yes, it *was* a man. Torn trousers were black with dirt; ragged shirt had no sleeves; feet were bare; black hair hung in two long braids; the face was dusky in the shadow, arms were folded, his bearing dignified. He stood without a motion. His own arms filled with wood, Gustaf straightened quickly. Over a great lump in his throat he asked, 'Who are you?' Hans heard and turned, staring.

'Big Whistle,' replied the man in a calm voice.

The boys were astonished. Big Whistle sounded like the name of an Indian. While in Red Wing they had seen a couple of Indians wearing 'store clothes.' They had seemed to be idle, shiftless men. This man, whose clothes were rags, had a proud manner. And though he had said only two words, he spoke them plainly.

'Where do you live?' asked Gustaf, amazed that his voice sounded so natural. His knees were shaking.

'West,' the Indian pointed. 'Where the sun goes

down,' he added as though they might not know. Still he had not moved. The three stared at each other; in the dim light it seemed like a queer dream. Gustaf's courage began to return. The stranger had no visible weapon. If he had wanted to kill them certainly he could easily have done it before they knew he was there. Gustaf set the armful of wood down and brushed the bits of bark off his sleeves.

'We live *there*' — he pointed to the campfire. The Indian nodded.

'Is your name *really* Big Whistle?' asked Hans. This meeting was one he had long hoped for, though, for a truth, the Indian didn't look a bit as he had expected one would. 'I never heard a name like that.'

For answer, the Indian unfolded his arms and put the fingers of his right hand to his lips. Instantly there was a whistle, a shriek, a terrorizing sound that echoed through the trees and beat back upon the ears. Hans was numb with terror. Gustaf's knees were weak as water; back at the camp Elna and the mother cried out in fear.

The Indian laughed gleefully. These were good people; they respected his big noise. He was pleased with the impression he had made.

'Big Whistle. See? No one make such big whistle.'

'I should hope not!' exclaimed Gustaf.

'Gustaf! Hans!' the mother called to them. 'Are you there?' Larsson and Ernst raced toward the grove.

'We're all right!' Gustaf answered. 'We're coming!' Then he turned to the Indian. 'Have you had your supper? We have eaten. But there is plenty for you.' He gathered up the wood he had dropped. The extra supply he'd meant to drag must wait till some other time.

The Indian collected an armful, too. Hans, not to be outdone, hastily scooped up all he could carry and the three walked toward the campfire.

'Big Whistle has not had his supper, Mother,' said Gustaf as they came near. 'Is there porridge in the pot?'

That was the best thing he could have said. His mother loved to be hospitable. She hardly glanced at the stranger as she poked the fire, ran for spoon and bowl, and stirred the left-over porridge. Larsson saw that the Indian was young, not much older than Ernst, likely; strong and straight. What was he doing *here?* The land agent had said no Indians were near.

Big Whistle accepted the bowl of porridge the mother handed to him, sat cross-legged before the fire, and ate every scrap. Not a word was spoken till the food was gone.

'Thank you,' he said gravely.

'You speak English well,' Gustaf remarked. Big Whistle grinned.

'Learn at school in Red Wing's Village.'

'You mean in Red Wing?' asked Larsson, to make sure he understood.

'Mean Red Wing's Village,' repeated the Indian firmly. 'White man say Red Wing. Right name is Red Wing's Village. Red Wing great Da-ko-ta chief. Wear headdress with white wing dipped in blood. Very handsome. Big Whistle Da-ko-ta, too.'

'Is that a tribe of Sioux?' asked Larsson, interested to be set right.

Big Whistle drew himself up; his eyes flashed angrily. 'White men are careless. Always say Sioux, Sioux! Indian is not Sioux.'

123

The Larssons stared, frightened by his manner.

'If Sioux is wrong,' said Gustaf, after a long silence, 'tell us, Big Whistle.'

'Sioux means enemy. Da-ko-ta is a great nation; seven tribes. Da-ko-ta Sioux to Chippewa, yes. Friendly to white man. Do not say Sioux to Da-ko-ta. Makes him mad.'

'Red Wing's Village was a Da-ko-ta village,' said Larsson. The Indian smiled, pleased as a child to know that his words were accepted.

'And you went to school there?' Gustaf suddenly thought about this. If an Indian could attend school there, perhaps a Swede could, too.

'Mission school for Indian,' Big Whistle answered. 'Seven, eight, nine snows past. Big Whistle learn to speak good English,' he boasted. 'Learn letters, too.' His English *was* good. The Larssons had noticed that. And he spoke so slowly and with few words; they could understand him.

'Is the school there now?' asked Gustaf.

'Mission gone. Gone five years. But Big Whistle learned.' To him, the closing seemed unimportant, now that he had learned.

An ember flared to brightness and shone on the faces around the fire. Quietly he rose and stood before them.

'Come again!' he said, and swiftly trotted into the night, leaving the Larssons staring after him, bewildered.

FISH AND HONEY

Chapter Sixteen

Big Whistle's departure was so sudden that for a few minutes the Larssons stared at the darkness into which he had vanished. Then the mother spoke.

'Where did he come from?'

'He was in the woods, Mother,' Gustaf explained. 'I bent down to pick up wood. When I stood up, my arms full, there he was, staring at me.'

'If Indians are going to pop out like that, I shall fear for the night to come.'

'Nonsense!' Larsson had been as amazed as any, but he did not intend to be fearful. 'Before we left Wisconsin we knew that Indians lived out here. Lange told us that only five years ago the United States bought these lands from the Dakotas.'

'But did you expect to see any on our own land, Father?' asked Elna. Her eyes were still dark with excitement.

'Swansson told me there were a few around. He said they were friendly and good trappers. Most of the tribes have been gone for several years. Only a few stayed on. He told me we might see one occasionally, though, to tell the truth, he spoke so lightly of it I gave the matter no thought. I remember now that he said to treat them as friends, if we saw any. You did right, Gus. You used good sense.'

Gustaf flushed with pleasure. Actual praise from his father was rare. 'I thought Mother would want to feed him since he had had no supper,' he said.

'Of course,' answered the father. His eyes sparkled with amusement. 'She is the one who has been telling us that Indians are just like other people; that we shouldn't be fearful of them.'

'That was before I saw one come so suddenly and make such a loud noise.' The mother was already ashamed of her fear.

'Big Whistle will know where to find game, Father. Maybe he will show me where to trap muskrat or beaver. Fur would be fine and warm to wear come winter; and we'll need meat.' Gustaf wished he had asked the Indian more questions.

'The boys in Vasa talked about stalking deer,' remembered Ernst. 'Maybe Big Whistle knows where deer winter.'

'Next time he comes we must learn more,' the father said. 'Now we need our rest if we are to do a good day's work tomorrow. Four days of my fortnight with the oxen are gone already and we have hardly begun. No more talk now.'

As he lay under the stars that night, Gustaf planned

126

all the questions he would ask Big Whistle when he came again. It was lucky they all knew enough English to understand the Indian. Surely he liked them and would come again.

But though the children watched every shadow, every tree, the days went by without a sight or sign of Big Whistle.

The work progressed. Six acres were plowed and dragged with the top of a half-grown oak tree. A furrow was turned around the entire one hundred and sixty acres. Larsson dared not keep the oxen another hour.

After dinner, Larsson and Ernst started for Red Wing. The father planned to go only to Vasa; far enough to see that Ernst understood crossing streams and avoiding marshlands. Perhaps he could buy a few supplies in Vasa. If he could get a cow, he would wait till morning to return. If not, he planned to return at once and go on with the work in the morning. Fields were plowed, but the seed should be planted at once.

Those left at home worked on the garden plot where carrots, turnips, and a few potatoes were already planted. In a tiny field, laboriously plowed with the hand plow, the mother had already planted flax. Now Gustaf and Elna dragged the plow along four more rows and the mother planted the seed.

As the sun dropped low, they took their ease, resting by daylight for the first time in many days.

On the grassy slope, Gustaf sat down, hugged his knees and looked around. The plowed field made a rich dark brown patch in the green landscape. In the small garden plot a tiny line of fresh green marked a row; likely that was the carrots his mother had planted the first day they worked. At his left, three walls of the sod house rose

127

seven feet high. Inside, the wall against the hill was dug straight and the dirt floor pounded hard. Behind, ridgepole and young saplings for rafters were cut and trimmed, ready for building the roof. There hadn't been an idle moment in the twelve days since they arrived. As he looked the place over, now, Gustaf wondered that they had done so much.

The mother took her kitchen knife and wandered away to dig some greens. The prairie was dotted with fresh green shoots, surely she would recognize something safe for eating; they needed greens. Elna tended the fire and stirred the porridge idly. Hans went to the creek to wash his feet and stayed to play with pretty stones.

Gustaf reluctantly rose to fetch the grub-hoe. His father had asked him to sharpen it and he had forgotten till now. He spit on the hoe and rubbed it against the stone. Lightly he touched the edge with his forefinger, to test it.

'Not bad,' he said to himself. 'But I'd better try it on some sod.' He stood up — and Big Whistle was there, beside him.

'You come quietly,' he exclaimed, startled in spite of the fact that he had been hoping for days that the Indian would come again.

'Indian never makes noise with his feet.'

Elna heard the voice and ran around the corner of the house, fearlessly.

'Now you will eat supper *with* us, this time,' she invited. How thrilling that he should arrive now, when the plowing was done. It made a kind of celebration. 'Though we haven't anything very good unless Mother finds some greens,' she added regretfully.

128

FISH AND HONEY

'Big Whistle brings his share,' said the Indian. From the pockets of his dingy trousers he pulled fish — two, four, nine fish. They slithered to the ground in a silvery heap. Elna stared. She hadn't tasted fish since the Prairie du Chien stay. These would make a fine supper.

'We fix.' Big Whistle gathered them in his two hands, but some slipped through. Gustaf laid aside the hoe and stone.

'I'll help.' He picked up the fish the Indian dropped and followed him to the creek. Walking thus, directly behind, he noticed Big Whistle's gait. He walked on the front part of his feet, almost on his toes; he placed one foot in front of the other; his moccasins made less sound than Gustaf's bare feet. With that straight, easy stride, likely he could go miles and not be weary.

Hans stared as they squatted down beside him.

'You came back!' His pleased grin was a welcome. 'Now you must stay this time.'

Big Whistle laughed. Drawing his knife from his belt, he slit and cleaned the fish so quickly Gustaf was amazed. Then he washed them and laid them on the grass.

'Big Whistle stay till moon comes up. Came to tell his brother about many things,' the Indian said then. But as they walked back to the fire Elna was tending, he was silent. What was it, Gustaf wondered, that the Indian had come to tell?

The mother returned soon, her willow basket full of greens, which she cooked with a tasty sour sauce. The Indian broiled the fish on stones he heated under the pot. They sat in a circle and ate, smiling at each other silently.

Gustaf turned over in his mind the many questions he

129

wanted to ask. But as Big Whistle ate in quiet enjoyment, it seemed rude to question.

Elna gathered up the empty bowls and took them to the creek. The mother tipped the porridge pot to make sure it was empty and lifted it off for cleaning. Hans sorted over the fish bones hoping to find one for a fish-hook. The sunset glow was peach-colored in the east and birds made bedtime sounds in the thicket. Gustaf and the Indian sat resting.

'Gus likes fish,' the visitor remarked. Gustaf nodded.

'I like to catch them, too. Where did you get these, Big Whistle? Will you tell me?'

'Yes. In big stream west there is wide rock, so.' He measured with his arms a rock some six feet wide. 'Gus go there to catch fish. After harvest moon Gus catch many fish. Now can catch enough.'

'Where is this big stream?'

'Three streams west.' Big Whistle spoke the English words so clearly that it was startling to hear his short, terse sentences. But it was easy to understand. 'One stream — see?' He pointed west where a low line of trees had already made Gustaf suspect the course of a stream. 'Next stream small and near. Then big stream and flat rock. Not too far. Gus can go in afternoon after work is done. Swede work too hard.' He laughed, but his eyes were kind.

'We have to work to get the crop in,' explained Gustaf. How could a person live without working hard? He had never heard of such talk.

'So white man thinks.' The Indian looked westward. The Dakotas had given up their lands in a hard-driven bargain because the white man wanted to come and till

130

the land. Was Big Whistle thinking of that? Gustaf
wondered, anxiously.

'Does Gus like honey?'

'Honey?' The question was a surprise. 'Of course I
like honey. Is there any here?'

'Yes, in big oak tree.' Big Whistle pointed southwest.
'Tree that lightning burned. Gus reach in and find
honey. Little sister and brother will like it.'

'Mother'll be glad to have some.' Gustaf sat up ab-
ruptly, eager to fetch some at once. 'Neighbors are coming from Vasa to roof the house, Friday. She wished she
had a sweet for the dinner. You show me where to get
the honey, Big Whistle, and she can make honey cakes.
Oh, thank you! She'll be very glad.'

'Friday? Gus get fish. Gus get honey. White mother
have plenty food.'

'Can't we go now?' Gustaf asked anxiously. The Indian stood beside him gracefully. Gustaf had a sudden
uneasy feeling that he might leave again.

'Mother!' he called. 'Big Whistle tells me where I
can catch fish like these he brought. And there is honey.
You can make cakes for the men.'

The mother hurried toward them, the freshly scoured
pot swinging as she ran. But Big Whistle would not be
thanked. Quickly he turned and ran. They saw him
against the fading rose of the sky, running in his easy
stride toward the west.

Chapter Seventeen

GUSTAF sat by the creek in the twilight, whittling a flute. Already, more than a month after Midsummer Day, June 21, the sun set noticeably earlier. Near-by, Brownie, the new cow, browsed idly. She seemed to like this after-supper time. Gustaf had milked her; soon he would tie

132

her up for the night. Brownie was a fine cow; she gave so much rich milk that the Larssons had butter and cheese as well as milk aplenty. Living was good now. And fine wheat was harvested only last week.

Gently Gustaf blew into the hole in the willow stick. Not deep enough. Big Whistle would scorn the tiny sound such a small hole would make. Gustaf poked with the tip of his knife to enlarge it. He felt awkward: his arms still ached after hours of working with the wheat.

His father had been in a dither about the harvest. Then, one morning, after days of anxiously watching the ripening kernels, he had hurried to the sod house, calling, 'Gus! Ernst! Come! The wheat's ready!' And harvesting began.

Larsson and Ernst cut the grain with scythes. Elna and the mother gathered the long yellow stalks and tied them into bundles. Gustaf stacked these in tidy stacks that would shed water if rain came overnight. The next day Gustaf and Ernst carried every bundle and made a large round mound on smooth ground east of the house. All that afternoon, Larsson, Ernst, and Gustaf tramped over that mound; over and over and over, loosening the kernels.

'Next year, we'll have oxen to do this part of the work,' Larsson promised. 'Wheat like this will make us rich. Go to it, boys! It's nearly all loose now!'

In mid-afternoon of that same day, they forked off the straw and stacked it near the place where they had started building a sod barn. Two large round stacks meant that Brownie would have plenty of clean straw all winter. The golden kernels, mixed with dust and chaff, lay on the ground and Larsson eyed the sky anxiously.

'We'll get rid of that chaff, come a wind. Tomorrow we cut rye.' Nothing seemed to tire the father, he was so excited by his wonderful harvest. The boys worked till they ached with weariness, and still there was more to do.

This morning, for the first time since the wheat was cut, there came a west wind. It blew steady and strong and burning hot from the prairies. Gustaf and Ernst spent the whole day tossing handfuls of wheat and chaff into the air, letting the wind blow the chaff away. The mother brought bread and cheese and a jug of milk out to them. Larsson wouldn't let them stop long enough to go to the house. The wind might die down any minute; he could hardly wait till the wheat was clean and bagged. Mid-afternoon, a thick layer of golden kernels, clean and full, lay on the bare earth. Larsson buried his hands in this wealth, then began measuring and bagging at once.

'It'll run forty bushels to an acre!' he gloated. 'We'll be out of debt in a year with a crop like this!'

'When will you sell it, Father?' Gustaf asked.

'That's the question, Son. I don't really know yet. Some say sell now; some say to wait. Prices may be higher. I guess I should take a sackful and go to Red Wing and get prices. But I'll talk to Pastor Norelius first. He gets around and knows what's best. We're lucky to know him — a godly man, but practical, too. Take this sackful along, Son. Better milk next, your mother'll be calling us to supper.'

Gustaf blew the reed again, this time rewarded by a shrill note. *Now!* That was more as it should be! Just shape the hole a little truer, wet it in the creek, slide the bark sheath back on and he could play a tune. Briskly he got up, tired muscles forgotten. He dipped the willow in the creek and shook off extra drops of water before putting it to his lips.

He played the 'Herdsman's Song' first — he knew that so well the notes almost played themselves. Fine! Now 'Star-Spangled Banner.' He had played it so often on his harmonica that he knew each note. It wasn't an easy tune; a real test for a homemade flute, for that tune needed a wide range. As the last note died away an echo seemed to come from the east, across the prairie. He paused, flute still at his lips, to listen.

Yes, there it was — amazing! The last strains of 'Star-Spangled Banner' far off eastward, the final note hanging on the evening air, clear and full. *That* sound was never an echo! Nor made with a home-cut flute, either. It sounded like an oboe. He hadn't heard an oboe since he left Sweden.

He ran up the slope back of the sod house and along the crest, peering through the deepening twilight. As he passed the clump of nut trees he spied a wagon, headed west. A great, handsome prairie schooner, pulled by two oxen. They were tired, he could tell by their walk.

'Settlers! More settlers!' This was the third time in two weeks that settlers had passed. His mother said the place would soon be crowded if it kept on! He ran to meet them. Big Whistle had been right when he said many new people were coming soon.

'Ahoy, there!' shouted the driver as he saw Gustaf. 'Any place where we can stop for the night?' The words were Swedish.

'You are welcome, sir! This is our home.' He pointed

to the sod house, its roof barely visible on ahead. 'Mother has porridge still hot from supper.'

Walking by the father was a boy, younger than Gustaf, a sturdy lad, his thick shock of yellow hair tossed back. On the seat of the covered wagon sat the mother, a girl about Gustaf's age, and a younger boy. A baby slept in the mother's lap. No one there had a horn. Whence came the music?

'I thought we'd turn up someone with all that noise,' laughed the father as he noticed Gustaf's enquiring look. 'Go round to the back of the wagon and you'll see 'Dolph, my wife's brother. He's been playing that oboe of his all evening. Don't know whether he plans to draw neighbors or frighten away Indians!'

By now, the Larssons had heard talking and the sound of the wagon and had come to make the travelers welcome. Mrs. Larsson stopped to poke the fire and set the kettle front before she came out of the house. She had heard Swedish words and knew she would have company.

'Edstrom's the name,' the traveler said as Larsson came near. 'I've a claim near here. Looks like good land all around.' His family climbed stiffly from the wagon, 'Dolph, a youth of eighteen or twenty, stepped from behind the wagon carrying his oboe under his arm.

'I brought it from Sweden,' he said to Gustaf. 'They told me I could buy *anything* in America and maybe that's true. But there's nothing like a Swedish oboe for carrying a tune. Nothing I like better, either — unless maybe hot supper!' He grinned, wiped off the mouthpiece carefully, and put the instrument back in the wagon.

'Make yourselves at home,' invited Mrs. Larsson.

'Elna, take them to the creek to wash. We haven't our well in yet, not till after harvest. Hans, fetch me wood, little sticks for a quick fire. Gus, you help them with the oxen.'

In a few minutes the Edstroms were in the house, the tiny room seemed packed with people; children climbed on the beds to make room for grownups. Mrs. Larsson thanked the good luck that brought Big Whistle yesterday with fine venison to exchange for cheese so there was meat pie, fit for company.

The men discovered that the Edstroms were to settle on the next section west. How thrilling to have Swedish neighbors, company for the children as well as for grown-ups.

'More families are coming from our province, too,' said Edstrom. 'We planned to take up land near together and make a settlement, like at Vasa. Nice for all of us. 'Dolph needs someone to tune up with. I see your boy has a flute. 'Dolph will like that.'

Mrs. Larsson hurried about, making them comfortable. The nearly finished sod barn hadn't been used, the men could sleep there on fragrant new straw. She was proud to lavish care upon these newcomers as the Pederssens had upon the Larssons last year.

'I couldn't buy a pair of oxen for love or dollars,' Edstrom complained as he unhitched. 'Had to rent. Now I'll have to drive these beasts back. Takes my time.'

'I might return them for you,' said Larsson thoughtfully. 'I plan to go to Red Wing soon. I want to sell some of my wheat. And Gus, here, wants to see about a job for the winter.'

'A job in Red Wing?' Edstrom was amazed.

THEY CAME FROM SWEDEN

'Aye, with a judge there,' said Larsson with a thrill of pride. 'My boy seems to want to be a lawyer.' Edstrom looked at Gustaf with new respect.

'To be a lawyer would be fine. Good for Gus; good for our countrymen. I wish I had had a lawyer who spoke Swedish when I took up my claim in Red Wing. It gives a man an uneasy feeling to sign a paper and not know the words written there. Though they say down in Illinois that the land agent at Red Wing is honest.'

'You're not new from Sweden?' Larsson was surprised at the mention of Illinois.

'We left Sweden in late winter. We rode the new steam train to Galena and outfitted there. Came up the river by steamboat. We meant to settle in Illinois near the river but Illinois is too crowded for me. More'n half the homesteads taken up; maybe all of them. If I cross the ocean to homestead, I want space. Like this.' He looked around the wide sweep of prairie, so still and beautiful in the sunset's afterglow.

'Maybe some of you would like to eat outside,' suggested the mother as they all crowded inside. 'The house seems small on a fine evening. We have bowls enough. I'll dish up the supper and you children sit on the hillside or down by the creek.' Proudly she counted out the wooden bowls Gustaf and his father had made, spooned porridge into each, and topped that with a generous serving of meat pie.

'Breta, step up and take your bowl,' prompted Mrs. Edstrom. 'The children are so tired from all the traveling and so many strangers it's no wonder they forget their manners. Axel, Levor, come and get yours now. Take your bowls outside as you're told.'

HARVEST

Shyly Breta reached for her bowl. Elna, with a sudden recollection of her own strangeness at the Pederssens', spoke quickly: 'I'll carry yours, Breta. Come on, let's go down by the creek.' The girls hurried from the house. Axel and 'Dolph took their suppers and followed Ernst and Gustaf out to where the new sod barn was going up. Levor and Hans tagged behind. Mrs. Edstrom tended the baby and the grownups sat at the table in the house, free to visit. Outside the long July afterglow faded into moonlight.

'Here's a sweet to finish' — Mrs. Larsson suddenly remembered she had some rye bread and a portion of honey in a jar. '*Elna!*' she called from the doorway. 'Come get the sweet and take it to the others. And tell them about Big Whistle; they'll like that. . . . I'll call again in a few minutes and you children must get to bed.' It sounded just like old times, in Sweden.

Chapter Eighteen

'MAY we go with the Edstroms, Mother?' Elna whispered
eagerly as the visitors made ready to leave the next morning. 'Gus and I could help them a lot.'

'Of course you could.' The mother smiled at her
daughter. 'But think how much you could help *here*.
Tell them good-bye nicely now, and later, when the work
is done, you may walk over and carry a surprise for their
dinner.'

Soon the visitors climbed into the great wagon and
drove off. Elna and Gustaf, thrilled with their secret
plan, said good-bye very cheerfully and then scurried
around quickly to get the chores done.

Gustaf fed and milked Brownie and turned her out to
graze; he led the pigs, two young ones and a sow Larsson
bought on his last trip to Vasa, away from the garden

plot and left them to hunt their own food in the meadow. Elna let the chickens (three hens and a rooster) out to graze. It was Elna's chore to watch the hens; to find the eggs laid somewhere on the prairie. The mother needed every egg for fall settings, and sometimes it wasn't an easy matter to locate them. Elna coaxed the hens in the direction of the grove and hoped the trees there would keep them from wandering too far. Larsson planned to get some geese, too. Those were fine for meat and fat and feathers, but today Elna was thankful there were only chickens to look after.

Larsson went with the Edstroms to help his new neighbor survey his claim and set the stakes. Edstrom didn't know English and he didn't know surveying. But he was a good judge of people; he was smart and honest and better supplied with money than most settlers. He would get along all right; Larsson could see that.

Before noon the Larsson place was tidy; the wood was chopped, water fetched from the creek. Gustaf and Ernst had worked most of the morning cutting barley; now sheaves were stacked in neat rows. The father would be pleased: it was hard for him to lose such a fine day in the middle of harvest.

'Gus! Ernst!' The mother shouted to them from the house and they ran toward her. 'You've done fine. You may stop for this day. After all, neighbors are as important to us as harvest. Come make yourselves clean and eat some dinner. That won't take long and you'll not be hungry when you get over there.'

The boys welcomed that call. They set the scythe and hank of twine by the house, washed themselves in the creek, and ate the food the mother had ready for them

'You carry this, Ernst,' she said. She handed him the heavy iron pot full of hot chowder, cooked ready to eat. 'Gus, you take the basket.' In it were fresh bread and a roll of cheese neatly wrapped in a napkin.

'Aren't we going, too?' exclaimed Elna as the boys started away.

'Of *course* you are going.' The mother laughed at Elna's worried look. 'You may carry a bowl of honey. There's just enough left. Hans will have enough to carry himself, for it is farther than you think. I declare! I believe I'll go, too. I can help them.'

Welcoming shouts greeted the little party as they approached the place there the Edstroms had made camp.

'I'm surely glad to see you husky boys!' shouted Edstrom over the greetings of the others. 'Neighbor Larsson and I have staked the claim but we need help with the tent. The mother, here, says she'll live in a tent till I build her a frame house. We need help to raise the canvas.' Ernst set the pot of chowder on the crane over the fire 'Dolph had going. Mrs. Edstrom put the coffeepot on and soon they were all eating. The Larssons, all but the father, politely declined their own chowder, but when the mother saw that there was plenty she made a little sign and they accepted small helpings. Chowder was delicious; much better than the plain porridge she had served them before they left home.

The great covered wagon was unhitched and many of the things it had held were scattered near-by. A great trunk, painted bright blue and decorated with flowers, stood open, revealing clothes, dishes, and a bright red glass compote. A long slender trunk covered with walrus hide was 'Dolph's, the children learned, inherited from his grandfather and fine for carrying the oboe and a few light tools. Blankets and gay coverlets were spread out to air. Now Mrs. Edstrom was eager to sit down and talk.

'We can work later,' she said cheerfully, 'and goodness knows we'll have to. But we haven't had good Swedish talk since we left the old country. Talk warms the heart.'

The men and boys stretched the canvas and drove stakes. Gustaf, Ernst, and 'Dolph hunted a straight tree, cut it down, and trimmed it clean for a center pole. In two hours the tent was up and the women bustled about settling possessions inside.

'We got this tent in Galena,' Mrs. Edstrom explained as she hung a gay quilt across one side to divide off a room. 'I got it the very day I first heard about sod houses. Though yours is very nice,' she added quickly. She had not meant to be rude. 'We shall build a frame house soon, I hope, and a tent will answer for a while.'

'You mean a log house?' asked Elna as she carried in a pile of plates. 'We're going to build one this winter.'

'No, I want a frame house with stylish weatherboarding, as they build them in the towns. There's a sawmill in Red Wing. I made sure of that myself.

'You and Breta may unpack all the dishes now and put them in the cupboard. It stands steady since Gus put wooden blocks at the corners.' Elna was fascinated with all the pretty things. Helping to unpack was as much fun as a festival.

Outside, the men planned the location of the sod barn.

'I'll get a cow and some pigs soon as I can,' Edstrom said. 'How about working for me a few days, Gus? You're a handy lad, I can see. I'll pay you twenty-five cents a day, if you come early. Ernst the same. Could you spare them to me, Neighbor Larsson? I want to plow a field and get in potatoes and carrots. They should ripen before frost. Winter wheat goes in, too; that new sort. You boys know how to build the sod barn and a storehouse for food. How about it?'

Gustaf dug his toe into the grass and looked at his father. Twenty-five cents a day! That was wonderful pay. In a fortnight he'd have a start toward the money needed for school in Red Wing. Larsson studied the matter.

'Suppose they come half a week, neighbor? Our harvest isn't all in yet and I need them myself. But we want to help you. They'll not take pay for the work.'

'They will if they work for me,' said Edstrom firmly. 'And I'll make 'm earn it!' He grinned at the boys good-naturedly. 'If they work, they deserve their pay and a thank you, too. We're lucky to find neighbors willing and able to help us.' So the agreement was made.

Going home, later, Larsson talked with Gustaf.

'I'm glad you can help Edstrom,' he said. 'And I can see it's fair enough that he should pay. The money will come in handy to you, Son. But we mustn't neglect the work on our own place. Neighbors so near, now, will make some difference. I had thought about some fencing but there seemed no hurry. With the next section taken, we'll have to be careful of the neighbor's rights. First thing you know, some day when we're busiest, Brownie or the pigs might wander into the Edstrom's garden plot. We need a fence. Then we can put the creatures to pasture without a worry.'

'To make a fence takes time, Father.' Gustaf hadn't thought of this new problem.

THE NEW NEIGHBORS

'Aye. But it will take Edstrom time to plant a garden and go to Vasa for stock, Son. We'll not worry ourselves. But we'll plan ahead.' They walked along thoughtfully. Larsson reached into his pocket and then held out his hand to Gustaf. In the palm were a dozen kernels of the new wheat. He had dropped them into his pocket after showing them to Edstrom. Gustaf took six and plumped them into his mouth. His father ate the others. The wheat was tasty, comforting to chew.

'The fence will be extra, Gus,' the father remarked as they neared home. 'Ernst is hiring to help 'Dolph plow. You are to cut sod for the barn. At home we'll get on with the harvest and roof our own barn. That fence is extra.' Gustaf didn't get his meaning.

'Tomorrow I'll stake out the pasture lot and we'll go over it. You know that clump of tamarack down the creek? Pastor Norelius says that's fine for the crossbeams but red cedar is best for posts. We've plenty of red cedar. Cut nine-foot posts; that allows a firm drop in the ground and high enough fence, finished. You get posts cut for the pasture and I'll give you two of the new pigs when they're born. Any two you pick.' He looked to see how his son would take this generous offer. Most fathers would have expected extra work without pay.

'Oh, *Father!*' Gustaf's eyes sparkled with pleasure 'You know you don't need to pay me. But if you are willing, I thank you. I'll tend the piglets carefully. Perhaps I could sell them in Red Wing to help pay for schooling and shoes. Books, too, maybe.'

'Aye. I'm thinking you will need all that. Norelius tells me that pigs are worth a lot in town. The country's opening up so fast there's not enough stock handy to

145

supply all who want to buy. Well, then, it's a bargain, Son.'

In a fortnight Larsson and Gustaf left for Red Wing. Many a day they had worked sixteen hours there was so much to do. Fine weather and a full moon allowed them to work a long day. Gustaf had contrived a drag on which Edstrom's oxen hauled potatoes and a few bushels of wheat. They started at dawn; with luck, they might be in Red Wing the next forenoon.

As they walked east, Gustaf talked about his hopes.

'Of course I know I can't stay in town this trip, Father. But if the judge still wants me, may I make plans for the winter? I'd not leave home till the fence is built and the work in shape. I can hardly wait till we get there Father.'

'I hope it will turn out well for you, Son. I want you to get ahead.'

At eleven the next morning they dragged into Red Wing. Main Street was a mess of mud from an early shower, but the sun shone now. People went about their business; a new sawmill nearer than the first one and a new sash and door mill hummed noisily. To a country boy, the town seemed full of activity.

'You run along and find the judge, Son,' the father said. 'I'll ask the agent where I should see about my grain and then I'll return the oxen. Meet you at the stable back of the hotel.'

The judge was not in his rooms, so Gustaf ran all the way to the Red Wing Hotel, nearly bursting to settle his business.

'Is Judge Turner here?' he asked the clerk in the hotel office.

146

'Not he! He's been gone ten days, now.'

'*Gone!*' Gustaf suddenly felt weak and sick.

'Aye. To St. Paul. He left on the *Itasca* early last week. He's got a big case up there with the railroad. St. Paul's getting to be quite a city.'

'When will he be back?' Gustaf could hardly say the words. His throat felt tight and dry.

'He didn't say.' The man stroked his whiskers thoughtfully. 'No, I don't recall that he said a word about coming back. He might decide to stay up there for all I know. He took his things.'

Gustaf knew that he should mind his manners and thank the man, but words wouldn't come. Blindly, his lips working but making no sound, he turned to walk back to his father.

Chapter Nineteen

PASTOR NORELIUS put the bridle on his horse's head, set
the saddle, and fastened the girth strap. Then he called
to his wife.

'If you have some food ready for me, I'll be on my way,
Wife. I plan to visit Larsson's place and two or three
others; I hope to be back in time to finish my sermon.'
Mrs. Norelius hurried from the cabin, smiling at him
cheerfully.

'I have only rye bread and cheese for you this morning.

148

Mrs. Larsson will want to give you dinner, if she has
enough, so you can make out. I hope they will let the
children come to school. It will mean a lot to them later
if they start this fall.' Mrs. Norelius wrapped the food
in a piece of homespun linen and tucked it into the left
saddlebag. The right-hand bag was reserved for the
Bible and Psalm Book the pastor always carried with
him.

'God be with you!' she said.

'And with you!' he answered, and started briskly on
his way.

How fortunate to have this gray horse, the pastor
thought, as he turned southwest across the prairie. With
only the tired old nag he'd had, traveling around the
country had been slow and difficult. The pastor had a
church in Red Wing. He took long missionary trips to
the northwest and served the church in Vasa. New people were coming out to settle each week, most of them
Swedish, and he should visit them and invite them to
church. He was burdened with duties. Then, only last
week, his congregation in Red Wing had surprised him
with the gift of this lively horse. Now he could get about
and work up the school in Vasa and make his calls.

'Larsson has three children who should be in school,'
he said aloud in his deep-toned voice. 'Gustaf seems like
a bright boy, from all I hear; Elna and Hans need schooling. They may think Hans is too young at the start;
Elna and Gustaf can teach him, once they begin coming.'
He studied over plans for caring for the children in Vasa.
When he rode up to the sod house, Mrs. Larsson was
down at the creek, washing. She noticed that a visitor
had arrived, dragged the wet things out of the water,

and hurried to see who had come. What brought a stranger here? she wondered.

The pastor knotted the bridle around a small tree and went to meet her.

'Mrs. Larsson?' he asked in Swedish. 'Is your husband here?' He was surprised at the quiet. He had expected a stir of family activity. 'I am Pastor Norelius. I was away, you remember, when you went through Vasa in the spring and I have long hoped for a visit. Have I missed him?'

'Good day to you, Pastor.' Mrs. Larsson dropped a curtsy respectfully. 'You honor us, sir. My husband will be back later in the day. The others are with him; they help the Edstroms roof the new barn. I would have gone over with them but my Hans cut his foot on a sharp stone this morning. It seemed he could not walk so far. They may come here for supper and music. Can you wait till then, Pastor?'

'No, though I wish I could. I will ride over to Edstrom's place and see them there. But the boy with the hurt foot, where is he? Can I do anything for him?' He turned to look, and spied small Hans standing in the doorway of the sod house. The mother had left him lying on the trundle bed, but he came to the door when he heard the sound of a new voice. Together the mother and the pastor walked up the slope to the house.

'Good morning, Hans!' the pastor called. 'So you cut your foot. Was it a clean stone?'

Hans, surprised at this question, looked round-eyed at the stranger. 'No, it was muddy from the creek. But Mother washed the cut with hot soapy water till it hurt. My foot is clean.'

150

Pastor Norelius nodded, approving. 'Does it hurt now?'

Hans looked at the pastor uneasily. The cut did hurt some. Far too much for Hans to care to run an errand. Often strangers wanted errands done, straw for a horse or water, maybe. On the other hand, the cut didn't hurt *much*. Hans wouldn't like to miss anything pleasant that the pastor might suggest.

'It hurts a *little*,' he decided. The pastor laughed and patted Hans's head.

'I want to see your father, Hans,' he said, 'and he is at Edstrom's place. Now, I have a horse tied back of the house. I wonder if you could ride over on my horse and surprise them. What do you think of that?'

'I think I could go,' said Hans quickly. 'I think my foot is about well now.'

'Fine! Then our only problem is to persuade your mother to pull the clothes quite out of the water. We don't want them to float down the creek to the river and down the little river to the Mississippi, and down the Mississippi to the Gulf ——'

'Truly, is *that* where the water goes?' demanded Hans. 'I wondered.'

'If you come to school in Vasa where we want you, there is much you can learn.'

'You must not bother the pastor with silly questions, Hans.' The mother spoke as soon as she could get in a word. 'I shall pull up my wash, Pastor, and we'll go at once. But do not bother with Hans. I was going to help with the dinner anyway. He can stay by himself while I guide you.'

Hans's face was a study. This stranger was a pastor; that was surprising enough. But to hear his mother suggest that he stay at home when he had been offered a ride, really *offered*, was too much. His lip quivered.

'Hans is big and brave,' said the pastor kindly. 'Of course he can stay alone.' Hans's heart plunked down to his hurt toe. 'But we need him. I plan to speak to the fathers about our school and Hans should be there with us. Come on, Hans! I'll set you on the horse and you can get the feel of it while your mother tends to her clothes.'

Hans barely limped when he went with the pastor to the tree where the horse was tied. The pastor tossed him high and settled him comfortably on the wide saddle. And Hans, in his delight, quite forgot that his new friend was a pastor and should be treated reverently. He laughed and touched the reins the pastor gathered up.

By the time they reached the Edstroms', Pastor Norelius was a good friend of both Hans and his mother. He had heard the story of their settling and of the coming of the new neighbors, as well as much earlier history of the family.

Arrived there, he set Hans down, tied up his horse, tossed off his coat, and took a hand at the job of roofing. The ridgepole was set; the trimmed saplings were in place, sloping evenly from ridge to wall. Now there remained the task of laying blocks of sod, each lapping a bit over the other on the saplings. The men were particular to set the sod with the lay of the grass downward for drainage. All winter the rain and snow would slide off; and next summer the grass roots would sprout and make a pretty green roof.

When the pastor arrived the men stopped work, but Norelius insisted on finishing the roof. He set to work at once.

A VISIT FROM PASTOR NORELIUS

Meanwhile Mrs. Larsson and Elna helped Mrs. Edstrom and Breta make a dinner worthy of a visit from the pastor. (It made no difference that they had never seen the man before; he was 'the pastor,' and as such any Swede would do him honor.) The girls fetched planks from the bottom of the wagon and set them across two carpenter's horses 'Dolph had made. Mrs. Edstrom opened the blue chest and took from it a handsome handwoven tablecloth of red- and white-checked linen and spread it over the planks.

'Now the silver, Breta,' she commanded. 'I haven't cleaned it since we came, I've been that busy. You and Elna must polish it for me. The powder is in the kitchen box. Don't be lazy, now!' She turned to Mrs. Larsson. 'It's lucky for me that Indian friend of yours was here only last night so I have plenty of meat. What ever do you suppose he took in trade? . . . No, don't wait to hear, girls. Breta can tell you all about it, Elna. Get at that silver quickly.' As the girls ran off, she continued the story to Mrs. Larsson.

'When he came, I was repacking some things in my trunk — linen and festival clothes and a bit of marble my cousin brought me from Italy. Edstrom, he laughed at me for bringing such a thing to America. But it was a pretty stone, so round and pink. I dropped it in a corner of the trunk when I packed, in Sweden. It was lying on the ground by me, last evening, when that Indian arrived with a great hind quarter of venison. Edstrom was to pay him. But that creature wanted my marble. So silly! Edstrom said to me, "Venison does us more good in Minnesota than a piece of stone, no matter where it is from." And that does make sense. So we bought all this' — she pointed at the venison proudly — 'for one round pink stone. Whatever an Indian wants with a stone when Minnesota is full of stones, I'm sure I don't know. But I am glad for the meat.' She talked on, delighted with all the flutter of preparation.

Elna carried the small roll of woollen cloth and the powdered pumice stone to the edge of a tiny lake, a kind of widening in the creek. She and Breta polished until the small silver bowl and two great hammered serving spoons sparkled in the sunshine. Breta's tongue ran on as steadily as her mother's; she told Elna about Big Whistle's strange choice of her mother's bit of marble no bigger than an apple, in payment for a large quarter of venison and a handful of fish.

'Mother wouldn't part with her marble and leave it in Sweden. Oh, no,' said Breta, giggling at the recollection. 'But she was so amazed that Big Whistle wanted it that before she thought she had said he could have it, and then there was no changing. He hurried away, pleased as though she had given him a fortune. I know he wanted it for some special reason. Do you know what it could be?' Elna had no idea.

Now the table was set for the men; wooden bowls and pewter spoons marked each place. The shining silver bowl, filled with store sugar, was near the end of the table where the pastor was to sit. Mrs. Edstrom counted the bowls and spoons and the log seats her husband had sawed; she was uncertain what to do about Gustaf. A glance at the work showed her that he sat astride the ridgepole setting the top rows of sod under the pastor's direction. He was working like a man. She set a place for him at the table. Hans and Axel could wait and eat later. Gustaf never guessed how suddenly he was promoted.

Mrs. Larsson turned the venison roasting over an open fire; fragrant odors steamed from the chowder in the cooking-pot. The girls set a crystal bowl of plum jam and the red compote filled with honey on the table. The small hand mill hummed noisily; Mrs. Edstrom had decided there wasn't quite enough meal for the dumplings. Cakes made with currants and spices brought from Galena were set out in a basket woven in Sweden. Coffee boiled up and the pot was pulled aside to settle the grounds.

Now the barn was finished. The men washed, came to the table, and stood by their places silently, while the pastor read from the Bible and prayed. They said grace together at the end of the long prayer.

This was a wonderful occasion, not only because the late summer sun was brilliant, the harvest good, the breeze warm and gentle. In that year, 1857, this party could have been given only in America. In the old country, the Larssons were cotters; the Edstroms, landholders. Elna and her mother might have gone in to help a neighbor, but only as servants. Larsson, Gustaf, and Ernst might have hired to build a barn, but not as neighbors. Even in the church there would have been a difference in station. Here they were equals, helping each other. One family had silver and pewter; the other had neither. But all had become Americans, with an equal chance to make home and fortune.

Then they sat down to eat. Elna and Breta dashed about with coffee mugs. The mothers spooned meat pie and dumplings. Between helpings the men ate rye bread and jam and honey. Everyone had a wonderful time, laughing, talking. Pastor Norelius thought of his little roll of bread and cheese tucked in his saddlebag and smiled. He didn't need it here.

Chapter Twenty

As THEY sat around after dinner was over, Pastor Norelius spoke to Gustaf.

'You are Gustaf, aren't you? The boy who wants to
learn to speak and read English?' Gustaf nodded and
came nearer.

'My wife told me about you. She said you had made a
good start last winter.' These sentences the pastor spoke
in English as a test.

'Thank you, sir. I do want to learn; and quickly as I
can. The coach driver and a neighbor helped me last
winter in Wisconsin.' He said the English words carefully to make sure of the sound.

'Wanting to learn is the first step toward an education,

157

my boy,' approved the pastor. Gustaf started to ask a question but the pastor said quietly, 'I shall speak to the others now. We'll talk more afterward.' Continuing in Swedish, he told them about the church in Vasa where he held services on alternate Sundays; about the school he had held for six weeks in the spring and hoped to open again soon, now that the snug log church was built.

'Minnesota Territory will have public schools before long,' he told them. 'Already school lands are set aside and a school tax planned. Schools will open in the towns first, of course, where more people will benefit. Teaching is in English, of course. Give your girls and boys a few months of teaching with a Swedish teacher and they will learn faster when they go to public school later. New language, new neighbors, new books and school all at one time slow a child's learning. You must prepare them for their opportunity to get an education in America.' He talked earnestly and with good sense.

'Can you spare your older boys for a couple of days?' he continued. 'We need them in Vasa to help us make benches and stools and cut firewood. With a fire for colder days, we can run the school for several weeks before severe winter begins. You may pay the small expense in money or in provisions; we need both. Bring cheese or a young pig or eggs or grain. Plan to send the children for three days a week. They can carry their food and we'll sleep them somewhere. On the week we have service Sunday, they may stay on and school will begin Monday; the other week, Tuesday. How about it? Breta? Gustaf? Elna? All of you? Do you want to come?'

The glad look in their eager faces gave him the answer. The children came close to ask questions and to hear what the fathers were asking the pastor. Wasn't it thrilling to have this happen so soon? They had wondered if a school might open in a year or two. And here it was.

Gustaf edged near the pastor. 'You say schools will open in the towns first, sir. Is there a school in Red Wing?'

'Yes, a nice school, built two years ago. The town took up a collection and built a good building; three big windows on each side. The building is better than the teaching just now, but we'll get good teachers as things settle down. And there is a college started, named for the Methodist bishop, Mr. Hamline. But the teaching in Red Wing is in English, of course. My church has a small Swedish school. Maybe you are ready for English, Gus; though I think Swedish this fall would get you along faster in the end.' Gustaf listened quietly, willing for the pastor to decide for him.

'Several new Swedish families have settled in Red Wing this season. I think now of a cabinet-maker who came from Winona. He has a son about your age. The name is Lindholm.'

'*Nels* Lindholm, Pastor? Perhaps he is the boy I fished with in Prairie du Chien.' Gustaf was so excited he forgot to speak in English; quick Swedish words rushed out and his eyes danced with eagerness. 'He is about as tall as I, sir, yellow hair and freckles across his nose.'

'Just like a dozen Swedish boys,' laughed the pastor. 'But now that I think on it, I believe the name *is* Nels. The family came from Illinois; stopped in Winona and then heard of a better opening in Red Wing. If you get to town, Gus, a friend will be fine. But a boy should not go to a town without a job or some good plan. Board and keep costs considerable. You can go to school in Vasa and get your start, then work out the other.'

Gustaf tried to forget the whole idea of going to town. He worked hard at home; put in three long days a week for Edstrom and went with 'Dolph and Ernst to Vasa to work on the furnishings for the school. He made a start on the fence posts. There was plenty to do.

A little more than three weeks after the pastor's visit, school opened. The cabin was clean and weather-tight. Two new tables and benches looked very handsome; the boys sat at one, on the right side of the room, the girls at the other, opposite. The teacher's table was against the wall, between. A small sheet-iron stove in the middle of the room was cold now, for the day was fine. Outside, wood was stacked ready to use when the weather changed. The pastor greeted nineteen girls and boys, more than he had hoped to gather, and gave each a copybook bought with money the fathers had contributed.

Gustaf opened his book quickly. Inside, the ruled pages were blank except for a short proverb at the top, printed in English, of course. He read a few: 'Handsome is as handsome does,' 'A rolling stone gathers no moss,' 'A penny saved is a penny earned.' The twenty lines below would soon be filled with copies made with the goose-quill pen he had sharpened that morning. At the back of the book were empty pages; the pastor explained that these were to be filled with Bible verses written in English.

Mr. Swansson had collected money from the fathers

and bought the teacher new books in town. Pastor Norelius showed them to his pupils; 'Webster's Speller,' that cost twenty-five cents; two 'Parker's Readers' each costing forty cents. With the Bible and Psalm Book and Catechism what more could a classroom need? he asked them. Shyly the girls and boys eyed each other. The pastor wrote their names in his book and school started.

At the end of the third week the pastor planned 'exercises,' and visitors crowded into the small room for the afternoon session to see how much the children had learned. Elna wished for her mother. Gustaf and Reuben Berg had been chosen as the two who had done the best work. When the time came for them to be examined and they walked front to the teacher's desk, Elna could hardly sit still, she was so proud.

'It's a good thing *I'm* not up there for the first exercises since we came to America,' she thought. '*I'd* forget all I knew.' Gustaf seemed very calm, though his eyes shone.

The two stood before the teacher's desk, each with his hands tightly locked behind. They bowed stiffly to the pastor, to each other, and then faced the audience. Of course they knew just what to do, for both Reuben and Gustaf had attended school in Sweden.

The room had never been so still.

'How many continents in the world?' the pastor asked Gustaf.

'Five, and Australia.'

'Correct. Name them, Reuben.'

'Asia, Africa, Europe, North and South America.'

'Correct. Bound the continent of Asia, Gustaf.'

Their geography answers were perfect. Neither missed

a word in spelling. They said their multiplication tables so fast and correctly the younger children could hardly follow them. Then came the most difficult test: the reading of a passage of the Bible in Swedish and translating it into English. The pastor had selected a well-known chapter, the Beatitudes; both boys knew these by heart and had practiced reading them in English. Gustaf pronounced the English words far better than Reuben; his accent, too, was good. He spoke without hesitation.

'You speak well, Gustaf,' said the pastor. 'Much better than Reuben.' Gustaf raised his hand and the pastor stopped, surprised at the interruption. 'Yes? What is it?'

'But, Pastor, perhaps the test is not fair. I studied English last winter.'

The corners of the pastor's mouth curled into a smile. 'The test is fair, my boy. Reuben has been over two years; he has been to school here. Tell your father you won the match today.'

Exercises ended with the singing of a Swedish song much like 'School is over, work is done,' and the children left for their homes.

As he hurried along the road, Gustaf passed Swansson, who called to him.

'Say, Gus! Stop by and get a ten-pound sack of wheat seed to carry to your father. It's the winter wheat Weatherby in Red Wing promised him; I brought it over in my cart. They say this wheat makes the best flour in the world; worth trying, I'd say. Weatherby will get the pay next time he comes out this way; he'll take it in grain or stock if your father prefers. He can sell stuff up the river and make money.'

Gustaf was glad to carry the extra load. They planned

162

to plow the next day; now the new seed could go right in and get a start before frost. He got the wheat, swung it over his left shoulder since he already carried a bundle of supplies over his right, and called to Elna that he was ready to go. She had waited for him. The Edstroms had gone an hour ago.

For a while they tramped silently, glad to be away from the village. Elna shifted hanks of wool for her mother that lay warm on her shoulder, and admired the geranium slip Mrs. Norelius had given to her.

'Maybe we can make a little pot for it, Gus, from the clay you discovered up the creek. Mrs. Swansson makes pots for her plants. She bakes them in her oven. Ellen says they crack sometimes, in baking; again they turn out fine. A pot with a geranium would look fine by the window, Gus.'

'Aye.' Gustaf's tone was absent-minded. They tramped on.

'I'll not be making anything till the posts are cut, Elna,' he said presently. 'I've only started them. Father wants that pasture fenced. I'm to get my choice of the new pigs, you know, for pay when the posts are all cut. I've the trees marked now, so I can work mornings and evenings before dark. A fence will be a fine improvement on our place.' He spoke as a partner, not a mere lad, helping with odd jobs.

All over the country settlers had been prosperous. Little of the terrible depression in the cities that autumn of 1857 touched them. Many a city man had put all his savings into high-priced land (as the man who bought the Pine Lake farm had done) and then lost all of it. Too many bought and could not resell. Immigrants

went west and took up cheap government land, worked
their own claims, as Larsson had, put in their own im-
provements; got along well, as the Larssons had.

'A fence is a fine thing,' Gustaf continued, walking so
fast Elna had to skip to keep up with him. 'I like getting
the pigs, too. It will give me a start toward an education.'

'Yes, it will,' agreed Elna indifferently. Imagine wanting *pigs!* She would a thousand times rather have a
dress made of store cloth.

'See how well Judge Turner did in Red Wing?' Gustaf
talked on. 'Now he has a big case in St. Paul, Mr. Swansson says. Red Wing will grow every year; or I might go
to St. Paul. Father says Minnesota Territory may become a state. I want to learn all the laws.'

Elna said nothing. Such serious talk made Gustaf
seem very grown up. She looked around, admiring the
scene; this strip of woods was pretty in the autumn. Out
on the prairie tall sunflower blooms were gone, the heavy
seed pods hung low. Goldenrod was rusty, its bright
color faded from the hot sun. Here, under the trees, it
still gleamed bright gold. Long graceful fronds of laven-
der cosmos swayed with a stir of air; purple asters with
golden centers were fresh, here; those in the meadow had
dried up in the last heat. Looking around to find more
flowers, she spied something moving.

'Gus!' she whispered in terror. '*Gus!*'

He glanced where she was looking. Then, quick as a
flash, dropped his load, grabbed her shoulders, and
pushed her down flat behind a great elderberry bush.

GUSTAF'S LETTER

Chapter Twenty-One

FOR a few seconds Elna and Gustaf lay flat behind the elderberry bush, afraid to move or breathe. The woods were silent. Not a bird chirped; not a breeze stirred a leaf. Surely no danger lurked near.

Moving slowly, Gustaf raised his head and peered through the bushes.

Some three hundred feet away a column of Indians walked silently in a circling direction. Gustaf counted ten, fifteen, twenty before he shrank down again, breathless. These were terrible-looking creatures, the most horrible sight Gustaf's eyes had ever seen. Stern faces were gaudily painted red and blue and green and yellow; bows hung over naked shoulders; quivers bulged with bright arrows; gaudy feathers thrust through headbands made the men seem like giants, tall and terrible. Some carried guns, awkwardly held. They were as unlike Big Whistle as a nightmare is unlike noon sunshine.

Marching silently, single file, the creatures passed by so near that if Elna had not happened to observe them she and Gustaf might actually have run into the line.

The children waited.

After a while Gustaf peered through the bush; then rose slowly and looked about. No one was in sight.

'They're gone, Elna,' he whispered, touching her shoulder. 'Perhaps this is the best time for us to run home, now, when we've just seen them go north.' He gathered up his load, handed Elna the wool and the geranium slip she had dropped.

Crossing the first meadow was a stern test of courage; they looked all around, then raced across to the woods on the other side. Soon home was only three miles away. At last they spied the sod house, smoke drifting peacefully from the chimney. It looked so *safe*.

The mother and father could hardly believe the fantastic tale.

'Maybe they were just a tribe going west for the winter,' the mother suggested. 'The pastor says they usually go for hunting.'

'You did right to hide quickly,' the father approved. He was deeply disturbed, but he did not intend his family to know that. 'Next time Big Whistle comes we'll ask him about all this.' But Big Whistle did not come. It wasn't till the next spring that the Larssons learned that Gustaf and Elna had seen a band of restless braves who went north determined on war. Goodhue County was lucky when they left, that autumn day.

Not knowing this, the Larssons were silent. The prairie, usually sunny and cheerful, suddenly seemed vast and fearful; the sod house, small and trifling shelter. Then the mother shook off her fear and spoke cheerfully.

'Now, you are not to worry. Supper is ready and you both must be starving with all that running and the great load you brought. You were a good lad to carry the wheat, Gus. That wool is exactly what I need, Elna. And the geranium is wonderful. We shall watch it grow. You were a smart girl to carry it so carefully.'

Supper was hot and good. Talk turned to school and news of the Edstroms. Indians were almost forgotten.

That was a busy fall. With three days each week taken out for school, Gustaf worked early and late when he was at home. Ernst now hired out regularly to Edstrom or one of the other settlers near. Several new families came that month and all needed help in building shelters before the winter cold began. Larsson bought an ox, a sturdy beast; Gustaf helped his father put in the winter wheat and they turned ten acres of fine land, ready for spring.

Some days Gustaf barely had time to cut one cedar; sometimes he cut several. He trimmed each one, dragged it to the lot marked off, and laid it along the line as his father had ordered. Nine-foot posts, they were, even and true. It seemed as though there never would be enough. But gradually the line lengthened. Seven weeks went by.

'You've almost enough, Gus,' Larsson remarked one day. 'We'll soon start setting them. I'll get Ernst to stay home and we'll make a day of it.'

167

'Then the piglets will be mine, Father.' Gustaf had made his choice, the fattest of the new litter, a black one, and one with white markings.

'You've surely earned them. But why you want pigs of your own, I don't see.'

'It will seem as though I had money of my own, Father; almost as though I hired out, as Ernst does. I can raise pigs and help you at the same time.'

Larsson nodded approval. Gustaf was a good boy. Strong and steady for his age.

The last post was dragged into place at dawn on a Tuesday morning, before Gustaf left for school. Much as he loved learning, he could hardly wait to get back home and claim his pigs. He planned to feed them well and keep them clean. Clean pigs might grow faster, he thought, though that was not the usual idea, then.

As he neared home, he ran ahead of Elna and went to the sty. Only seven of the nine new little pigs were there. The two he had chosen, the best of the litter, were missing. Gustaf's mother ran toward him from the sod house.

'Were they sick?' he called anxiously. 'They looked fine last Tuesday.'

'No. It's Weatherby, Son. Your father couldn't help it.'

'Weatherby?' Gustaf stared at her. What had Weatherby to do with his pigs? Then he remembered the wheat.

'But Father had decided to pay him in money. We need the stock ourselves. Anyway, those two were mine. Father said so.'

'Aye, Son. I know it. And your father handed him the money Swansson said was right to pay. But he wouldn't take it. Once he saw those pigs he wouldn't touch the money. Your father couldn't make him understand that those two pigs were yours.' She wiped her eyes on the corner of her gray apron; the matter worried her. 'If *you* had been here, Son, *you* could have talked to him.' Tears rolled down her face. Pigs all looked much alike to her, but she knew Gustaf had taken a notion to those particular pigs and had earned them fairly.

Gustaf roused himself. Never in his life had he seen his mother cry. And, after all, the pigs were gone. Might as well make the best of it.

'Never mind, Mother. The debt is paid now and Father will like that.'

'But he feels badly, Son. Likely Weatherby would have taken other pigs if your father could have made him understand. It's a great pity.'

Gustaf patted her shoulder with awkward tenderness. Then, making the excuse that he must put his bundle away, he went around to the other side of the house and sat down on the slope, hugging his knees thoughtfully, his eyes misted. He must overcome this childish disappointment.

A touch on his shoulder made him hold his breath.

'I couldn't help it, Son. I guess your mother has told you. I didn't know the English words to make him understand that those two piglets were yours.' The father sat down by Gustaf silently. 'I can see that it is different here in America,' he continued presently. 'Most of the people coming to Red Wing are Americans. They speak English. It is only around here and in Vasa that I can do good business in Swedish. I see now that it isn't enough to come to a new country, Gus. We have to make

169

ourselves into Americans; learn the language and American ways. You were wiser about it than I.'

The son stared at his father, eyes suddenly dry and bright. Need of education, then, was not just a notion of his own. His father thought the idea important, too. He edged over closer as his father sat beside him.

'We're making good progress in school at Vasa, the pastor says. I can read almost well enough to go to an English-taught school. He told me that today.'

'I'm proud of you, Gus. I was thinking you might *t*art to teach me evenings. But now I expect you'll be going.'

'Going? Where?'

'Didn't your mother tell you? I guess she was so worried about the piglets. There's a letter for you in the house. Weatherby brought it. He says the pastor was talking to Judge Turner about you; he calls you a fine boy, Son.'

Gustaf hadn't waited to hear the end of the sentence. He sprang up and ran into the house. Yes, there was a letter, set on the shelf his father had pegged into the sod wall, above the table. The paper was white, folded in half; the edges sealed shut with bright red sealing wax.

Gustaf took it down and turned it in his hand as his father and mother came into the room.

'It says "Gustaf Larsson," as though I was a man. I wonder what is inside.'

'Maybe you'd better open it, Son,' suggested his father kindly. The mother stood in the doorway, twisting the corner of her apron round and round into a knot.

Gustaf gently cracked the seal and spread the paper open.

GUSTAF'S LETTER

Dear Gus [it said]: Eric Norelius says you haven't forgotten our talk last spring. I'm back from St. Paul and plan to stay in Red Wing this winter. I could use a bright boy to clean my rooms, tend my horse, keep my fire going, and run errands. I would give him board and keep. How about it? School is free but you need some cash if you want to come, for books and other things. We might raise it selling grain if your father is short on cash. Wheat sells for a dollar fifteen a bushel right now. If you want the place, come next week.

Yours res'f'y

Eli T. Turner

Gustaf had read the letter aloud, but a glance at his parents reminded him they had not understood. He quickly told the meaning in Swedish.

'May I go, Father?'

'Aye. It's your chance. But we'll miss you, Son.'

Elna ran into the room. She had been hunting eggs with Hans. 'Miss who?' she wanted to know.

'Gus is going to work for Judge Turner and attend school in Red Wing,' said the mother. 'It's all settled.'

'Must I walk all the way to Vasa alone?' demanded Elna.

The mother laughed and ruffled her yellow braids. 'Don't the Edstroms go any more, Elna? But you'll have a brother for company, don't fret. Hans starts next week. Eight miles is little to walk for an education, and he might as well begin. Grownups are planning to learn, too. Your father will get the Edstroms and the Vanbergs to study evenings. We're going to be Americans. It's high time.... Gus, you'll need store shoes and a new shirt,' she suddenly remembered.

171

'I've got some money in the brass box, if you can spare that, Father. Perhaps I can earn some in Red Wing, after I get there.'

'You're going to start out right,' said Larsson. He had been thinking hard. 'I'll give you five dollars and two pigs. Take your pick. They're good, Gus, even if you hadn't chosen them. You can carry them in a sack when you go.'

Elna giggled. 'Gus will "Squeak, squeak!" all over the prairie. Will you mind, Gus?'

'Not I!' Gustaf laughed at her fancy.

'Better not waste time on foolishness, Elna,' the mother reproved briskly. 'You must finish Gus's new socks by Monday. I have to make him a shirt and mend his coat. This family has work to do.'

Gustaf folded the letter and put it back on the shelf. It looked very impressive there. He took off his school coat and picked up the bucket for milking.

'It seems to me, Father, Weatherby didn't do badly by us in coming even though he did take my piglets.' The father grinned. The Larsson family was doing well, for a fact.

THE FIRE

Chapter Twenty-Two

GUSTAF put a stick of wood in the stove, turned the damper halfway, and went back to his work. 'Davis's Arithmetic' was spread open on the table and beside it, a slate covered with problems. Gustaf checked each answer, then laid the slate aside for the judge to see when he returned. Before starting on his history lesson he leaned back, relaxed, and looked thoughtfully at the glowing fire in a base-burner. Even now he could hardly believe all that had happened recently.

THEY CAME FROM SWEDEN

The trip to Red Wing had not been easy; two young pigs in a sack made complications. They squealed, as Elna had predicted. But their squirming was more bothersome than the squealing. Gustaf had folded his blanket over one shoulder and swung the sack over that; he carried his winter coat on his arm. Pockets were filled with food for himself and corn meal for the pigs; the mother had tied the meal tightly, but it was quite a pocketful. At dark, he stopped by a little brook and laid the sack on the grass. Carefully he pulled one little pig out, tied its forefoot with stout twine, and knotted that around a sapling. Then the second piglet got his freedom the same way. They squealed happily and rooted in the grass while Gustaf mixed a soft mash of the corn meal for their supper. He ate his bread and cheese and fried fish and rolled into his blanket to rest. The pigs were a big responsibility; he didn't sleep much.

Early the next afternoon he came in sight of Barn Bluff, the great limestone cliff just south of the town, and before long he was walking up Main Street in Red Wing. Judge Turner welcomed him and within an hour had sold the piglets at a good price.

'Might as well get you some store shoes, Gus,' the judge decided. 'Your wooden shoes will look odd in school. They're noisy, too. You might as well start right, now that you have the money.' By the time Gustaf had walked along the rough plank sidewalks to sell the pigs and go to the store for the shoes he was embarrassed by the noise his clods made and the way people stared at him. The new shoes were very handsome; he was glad he had them when he went with the judge to Mrs. Allen's boarding-house for a good hot supper. After that,

THE FIRE

Gus would cook his own breakfast and supper in the judge's rooms and have dinner at Mrs. Allen's — and a very generous arrangement for a poor boy, the judge's friends thought.

As they walked back after supper they met Nels Lindholm on the narrow sidewalk. Nels was doing an errand for his father and nearly stepped off the planks into the mud, he was so surprised and pleased to see Gustaf. The judge waited, interested, while Gustaf explained how he happened to be in Red Wing and the boys agreed to see each other at school.

But, as it turned out, Gustaf was accepted in the town school and started his work in the Fifth Reader. Nels, who had learned very little English, had to go to the church school a while longer, till he was ready for the town school. For the first few days Gustaf felt very lonely; the children stared at him; he didn't know the ways of reciting, nor any children. But he had soon learned. And already he felt at home in these rooms over the dry goods store.

He opened his history book, Willard's 'History of the United States,' and began to read. Outside the wind howled. He thought of the small sod house on the prairie; a sod house was warmer than a frame one, in town, on a November night like this. The north window rattled; a wedge of wood would stop that clatter. He picked up a bit from the woodbox, walked across the room to set it in the window frame — and stood stock still, hardly believing the sight he saw.

Bright tongues of flame curled out from the eaves of the barn back of the hotel and flared quickly in the wind. The loft over that barn, Gustaf knew, was filled with crisp new hay. (It was the same loft that the Larssons had lived in last spring.) It would burn in a flash; and in a stall underneath was Judge Turner's new bay horse.

Grabbing his coat, Gustaf dashed down the stairs shouting, 'Fire! *Fire!* FIRE!' as he raced up the street. Heads popped out of windows; voices asked, 'Where?' There was no time to answer; Gustaf had but one thought. He must get that horse out. Lucky he knew the latch, it was a tricky one. He hurried inside. Already, not two minutes since he had stood at the window the whole top of the barn was in flames. The hotelkeeper's cows bellowed. Several horses stamped and whinnied. Travelers, stopping at the hotel, stabled their horses here. Tonight there seemed to be several. Now people began to come.

'Get the pump going!' shouted one.

'Bring all the buckets you can find!' called another.

'Where's the new Fire Department?'

'They're coming up the street now. Hear 'em?'

'Nice Ranger! Good Ranger!' Gustaf was in the barn, in Ranger's stall now, patting his flank, speaking in a quiet voice. Shaking off his coat, Gustaf threw it over Ranger's head and tied the sleeves tightly under his neck. Then he loosened the halter, backed Ranger out of the stall, and led him to the door.

'Nice Ranger. Good Ranger.' Now they were outside. Now across the lot. Now Ranger was tied to a post and Gustaf, relieved, took the coat off the horse's head.

'Boy! I've two horses in there! Can you get 'em out for me? Just my luck to get in an hour ago on my way to St. Paul,' he added.

176

'I've got a horse and a pony, myself,' shouted another. 'Give you a reward if you'll get them out for me!'

Gustaf needed no reward. He thought of the horses under that furnace. He dashed back into the barn. The Swiss was there, trying to get his cows.

'Cover their heads!' Gustaf shouted to him. He threw his coat over the nearest horse, led it out, and handed the bridle to the man running by. Now another one. Two men ran in, picked up the pony, and carried it out, kicking and whining as it was. Someone fetched blankets; now the cows were out. The animals went meekly enough once their heads were covered, but some of the men seemed not to know that trick. Gustaf came out with the second of the travelers' horses just as the volunteer Hook and Ladder Company arrived and took charge.

'Don't waste water on that barn!' shouted Captain McIntire. 'It's a goner. Save the other buildings.' He scattered the men; sent two to climb on each neighboring roof and soon had bucket lines going. Now if the well held out they might save the stores, but in this wind, it wouldn't be an easy fight. The barn roof crashed, and by its brilliant light Gustaf saw Nels and his father pouring water on the hotel roof. Sparks whirled and people scattered. Then the barn's ridgepole settled down, the glare faded. The danger seemed over.

'How much did you save?' someone asked the hotel man.

'My cows, thank goodness. They give me the best butter I've ever had.'

'Get all the horses out?' another asked.

'Well, there stand four and the pony. I reckon that was all there were tonight.'

'Where's that boy who led out my horse?' asked the

man from Chicago. 'Smart lad. I wouldn't have risked my neck in that inferno. But I'm glad to have my horse.'

'That's Gus Larsson from over beyond Vasa,' said the hotel man. 'He's right here.'

But Gustaf had gone. As soon as the animals were safe he began to figure on a place for Ranger. He couldn't risk leaving him there. If the fire spread, the horse might break his halter and run. When the loft crashed, Gustaf stood by patting him and talking softly to quiet him. What should he *do?* Then he remembered an old empty cabin he had seen down near Barn Bluff. It was one of the three buildings that formed the mission, years ago. Big Whistle had told of it; that was why Gustaf had gone to see it one Sunday afternoon.

He untied the halter and quietly led Ranger around the hotel, away from confusion. No one noticed them go. Ranger stopped trembling now, and followed meekly.

After the glare of the fire the street seemed very dark. Gustaf closed his eyes and waited a second. Ranger nosed his shoulder — it hurt! He reached around enquiringly. There was a hole in his shirt and his shoulder was burned. And *where* was his coat?

'Ranger,' he said, walking on, 'I'll put you in the cabin. Then I'll run back and find my coat. Can't lose a coat this time of year.' Now they reached the cabin. Gustaf kicked open the door, walked inside — and stepped on someone who jumped up with an angry snarl.

'Get out of here!'

Gustaf was amazed. Big Whistle had said this cabin was never used.

'Get out! This not your cabin!' A great relief spread through Gustaf.

THE FIRE

'Big Whistle, this is Gus.'

'Gus?'

'Yes, Gus. I came to town as I told you I hoped I could. You didn't come back.'

'Gus.' Arms reached out in the dark to touch Gustaf. 'Yes, it is Gus.'

'Of course. And how comes it you are here when there is a fire in the village?'

'It is not my fire,' said the Indian coldly.

'Nor mine. And I think it's out now. I thought to put the judge's horse in this cabin, for the night is cold and the barn is burned. Where shall I put him, Big Whistle?' Ranger, hearing voices, thrust his nose into the doorway and Gustaf patted him.

'Horse can stay here. Big Whistle goes west with his brothers. Leaving now.'

'Oh, thank you, Big Whistle. Must you go right now? I have lost my coat. Could you wait with Ranger while I fetch it? I need that coat this winter.' No answer.

Gustaf was surprised. He had expected his friend would agree quickly.

'Big Whistle stay,' the Indian spoke slowly. 'Be quick, Gus. White man not like Indian.'

Gustaf was astonished. What did the white man's liking have to do with staying there a few minutes?

'They'd like you if they knew you, Big Whistle. They do not know you are here, maybe.' Suddenly Gustaf thought to be curious about that himself. 'Why *are* you here?'

'Run for coat, little brother. I watch horse. Come back soon.' He took the halter and spoke gently to Ranger, coaxing him to bend his proud head and come into

179

the small room. Gustaf dashed off, his burn forgotten.

The Fire Department was still working; a blaze on one
roof threatened a whole block of stores. But Gustaf
dared not stop; Ranger was his responsibility. There
seemed plenty of men and boys for the work. He hurried
to the post where he had tied Ranger and searched
around in the darkness. Yes, there was the coat. Relieved, he picked it up and was hurrying away when a
voice caught his attention.

'Big Whistle, they say he calls himself. I saw him
slinking around about dusk.'

'He's a decent Indian,' another voice said. 'He went
to the mission a few years ago. He wouldn't set a barn
afire.'

'I wouldn't trust any Indian as far as I could throw a
bull by the tail,' said the first voice angrily. 'The barn's
burned. An Indian was in town. I can put two and two
together if you can't. I mean to find him.'

Gustaf waited to hear no more. His coat tucked under
his arm, he dashed down the street to the cabin, dark
under the shadow of Barn Bluff.

A REWARD

Chapter Twenty-Three

'BIG WHISTLE!' Gustaf dashed into the tiny cabin. 'You must go!'

'Yes.' The Indian spoke quietly.

'They say you set the barn afire!'

'Does Gus think Big Whistle burned barn?' the Indian demanded coldly.

'No! How silly! You wouldn't do such a thing.'

'Gus good friend.' From the darkness a hand reached out and grasped Gustaf's shaking fingers. 'Gus is right. But other people will blame Indian.'

Gustaf was silent. He had heard what was said.

'Do you know how it caught fire, Big Whistle?' he asked, and waited long for the reply. But when the Indian finally spoke he did not answer that question.

'Big Whistle going west. My brothers go north to fight the Chippewas and white men. Mission school taught Big Whistle not to go on warpath. Plenty good living by fishing and hunting. Plenty good land west.'

'Yes, that's so,' said Gustaf, wondering what all this had to do with the fire. Ranger stamped and Gustaf patted him. 'Good Ranger! Quiet, now.'

'Big Whistle came to Red Wing's Village to leave tribute at Chief Red Wing's mound,' continued the Indian. Gustaf knew the place where some said the chief was buried, high on the crest of Barn Bluff, overlooking the long stretch of the Mississippi. Only last Sunday afternoon, he and Nels had climbed up to see it, and wondered at the stones piled in a heap.

'Tribute?' he asked.

'My tribute. A pink stone, round as the full moon in harvest time,' answered Big Whistle. 'At twilight I laid it there. Now Big Whistle goes west.'

'So that's what the pink stone was taken for,' Gustaf thought to himself. 'I must tell Mrs. Edstrom.' Suddenly he remembered the accusation made against the Indian.

'You must go quickly, Big Whistle. Now, this minute.'

'Gus speaks wise words. I go.'

'But first tell me who set the barn afire.'

The door was half ajar, but the Indian paused.

'Big Whistle on bluff. Saw white man come from boat. He walk up street; very uneasy. He go in barn. Smoke come from his pipe.'

A REWARD

'You think he went up to the loft to sleep and his pipe set the fire going? You think that was it, maybe?'

'Big Whistle knows what he saw. Indian does not "maybe." Man went in barn. Barn burned. Now I go.'

The old leather hinges whined as the door opened. For a second the tall Indian stood, outlined against the sky over the river. Then Gustaf was alone with Ranger. The horse switched his handsome tail impatiently, and stamped his right front foot.

'Good Ranger. Wait, I'll see if anything here might hurt you.' Gustaf groped around the tiny room and made sure the cabin was empty. On the floor was an accumulation of leaves, chips, dirt, soft enough to bed a horse.

'Lie down, Ranger. Lie down.' The horse was restless, keyed up by the fire and the strange room. Gustaf talked to him quietly a long time before he settled down. Worn with excitement and the pain from his burn, the boy finally dropped into a doze, too.

A streak of sunlight under the door wakened him. He rubbed his eyes and shivered. It was cold as all out-of-doors. He'd better hurry and make the fire for the judge. He started up, Ranger snorted — and Gustaf remembered everything. Stiffly he got to his feet, shook off dust and dirt, and opened the door. Ranger scrambled up, too, nearly knocking out the side of the old cabin in doing so.

'I wish Judge Turner was at home,' said Gustaf. 'I don't rightly know what to do with you, Ranger. First we'd better go up town and see what's going on.' He eased Ranger out of the small door, tossed his coat over his well shoulder, and started up Main Street.

183

To his amazement nearly a block of stores had burned. The embers on the roof had not been put out as he'd supposed. The town looked strange in the morning light. Gustaf hardly knew how to find a place to keep Ranger; and his shoulder hurt. Where could he find a patch to mend his shirt? He couldn't go to school Monday with a hole like this. The judge had expected to get home this noon, but sometimes he was delayed. Gustaf wished for his mother, and the thirty miles seemed very far to be away from home.

Ranger jerked at the halter and pranced. Up the street, near the burned stores a crowd of people stood idly looking at the damage done. Someone heard Ranger's quick step.

'There's the boy who got out the horses!' the one who turned to look shouted. And before Gustaf knew what had happened he was in the midst of a friendly group who shook his hand and said words of praise.

'You're Judge Turner's boy from out in the country, aren't you?' asked one.

'Lives over Albright's store with the judge,' said another before Gustaf could reply.

'Look at his shoulder! You need some salve on that, Son,' said a third.

'Mrs. Albright'll fix you up. She's a cracken good nurse!' They turned toward the Albright store. Mrs. Albright spied them through the windows and hurried out.

'Gus Larsson, you come right in here. Tie the horse to the hitch-post. He'll be all right for a while. What's the matter with your shoulder? Got a burn? I'll fix it in a jiffy. Give you breakfast, too. I'll wager you've not had a bite.'

A REWARD

'You're right, ma'am,' said Gustaf. He reached for his cap, to take it off politely, and suddenly remembered it was up in his room. 'I had Ranger to look out for. The only place I could think of to keep him safe was the little cabin at the old mission. I thought the fire was out.'

'So did everyone else. That's why the town nearly burned down. Sam!' she shouted out the back door of the store to her husband at the woodpile. 'Gus is here; burned and hungry and the judge's horse not hurt a mite. Gus is worried about feed; I see it in his look. Can't someone hand out a sack of oats till the judge gets back?' She bustled about in her kindly New England way and soon a smoothing salve took the sting out of the burn; a soft linen bandage protected it and Gustaf sat down to a great bowlful of hot porridge covered with rich milk.

'Where do you think I'd better keep Ranger, Mis' Albright?' asked Gustaf presently. 'The judge hoped to get back at noon but he's never sure. If that man hadn't had a new buckboard he wanted the judge to ride in, he'd have taken Ranger for the trip.'

'And with a contraption like that you can't tell when they'll be back. Might lose a wheel going over a creek easy as anything. Then they *will* be in trouble!' She laughed good-naturedly and set a dish of honey by the porridge. 'Spoon some of that for yourself, Gus. A person needs sweet when he's been cold all night. Now about Ranger. Why, it's a good day; why not leave him hitched right where he is? If the judge is not back by night, ask Whitlock. Maybe he'll let you put the horse in the shed by the brickyard. That makes a fair shelter for this time of year.'

185

'The judge is particular about Ranger,' said Gustaf, doubtful of the shed idea.

'You seem to be, too,' she laughed. 'He'll be pleased with your work last night.'

'I got through all the problems he set me, but I hadn't started on the history.'

'What's that?' She stared at him, amazed at the reply.

'When he goes away, he sets me problems. That helps me catch up with the class. Isn't that what you meant?' Gustaf paused, spoon halfway to his mouth, puzzled by her look.

'Listen to the boy!' she exclaimed to the two men who just then came into the store. 'I tell him the judge will be pleased with his work last night and he thinks I mean *arithmetic!*' She laughed till she had to wipe her eyes on her big calico apron.

'This the boy who discovered the fire?' demanded one of the visitors. Gustaf looked up at him. Long whiskers covered the lower part of his face; his eyes were bright blue and friendly. He wore great high boots and a heavy woollen coat, belted, with a short gun thrust through the strap.

'I — I happened to look out and see a flame, sir.'

'What's your name, Son?' the second man asked. He came close to the counter behind which Gustaf sat, the nearly empty bowl of porridge before him.

'Gustaf Larsson, sir.' He rose respectfully.

'That's the name the Swiss mentioned,' the first man said. 'Son of a Swede who came out to homestead. Well, Son, my partner and I are obliged to you for saving our horses. We need them. We're on our way to Fort Snelling now.'

A REWARD

'You are very welcome, sir.' Gustaf spoke his best English, proud that he could say the words as the American spoke them. 'I didn't save all. Others helped, sir.'

'Oh, we understand you didn't do much,' the big man grinned at Gustaf. 'You only discovered the fire and got out two of our horses besides waking the town. The fire would have ended with the barn, too, if anyone had stayed awake to watch it.' He came closer.

'Did you ever want a pony, Son?'

'A pony?' Gustaf didn't know what to make of such a question. 'I don't understand.'

'Well, my partner and I aim to pay our way, and you surely saved us three good horses even though you pulled but two of them out of the barn with your own hands. We've got a good Indian pony out here; took it in a trade and haven't any real use for it. If you think it's worth feeding, it's yours.' Gustaf stared, his throat working strangely. A pony. He couldn't speak.

'Of course he'd like a pony, stranger. Any boy would.' Mrs. Albright came to the rescue. 'And as for feeding, oats aren't going to cost too much when a boy like Gus buys 'em in this town. He'll manage, thank you, or my name's not Lucinda Albright.'

'You mean the pony would be mine, sir?' asked Gustaf. 'All because I happened to stand at a window and see a fire?'

'The pony is yours, Son. But the reason is a mite different. It's yours because *when* you stood at a window and saw a fire, you did something besides stand there!' He laughed heartily and reached for Gustaf's hand. 'That pony'll be a lot more use to you than to us. It's hitched up the street by the hotel. Well, good-bye.'

187

THEY CAME FROM SWEDEN

'I thank you, sir, I thank you! I thank you!'

'We're both pleased. That's the way it should be, Gus. Well, we'll be going.'

The strangers walked down the wooden steps to the street, mounted their horses, and rode north. The third horse, led by a stout halter, was a 'spare,' it appeared.

'Thank you, sir!' Gustaf called after them.

The big man turned to grin at Gus. 'Good riding!' he called. And they were gone.

'Who are they?' someone on the street asked.

'City men. Going to Fort Snelling.'

'They talk of opening some mining claims way up north,' said another.

'Good idea, if they don't get into trouble with the Chippewas.'

'They surely played fair with our Gus. The judge will be pleased.' The words were warm and friendly.

'If you'll excuse me, ma'am, I'll see my pony,' Gustaf said to Mrs. Albright.

'Run along,' she replied cheerfully. 'There's another hitch-post out front. Bring your pony here where you can see him, Gus. Then come back and eat some more breakfast. I'll wager you're not filled up yet. What do you think of it all, anyway?' she added kindly.

'If it's really true that a pony is mine' — Gustaf still didn't quite believe — 'I think my family will be surprised. *Me* with a pony!'

AN UNEXPECTED TRIP

Chapter Twenty-Four

JUDGE TURNER and his client, riding in the stylish buck-board, arrived in town about noon and were amazed at the sights they saw. The hotel barn was gone, half a dozen stores were damaged by fire, and Main Street swarmed with a confusion of people, cows, and pigs. Men were far too interested in talking to attend to every-day duties. People gathered around the buckboard and told the story before the judge had time to climb out. He listened, grunted approval, and as soon as he could get away hurried up to his rooms. There he found Gustaf, mopping the floors in the regular Saturday cleaning.

'Well, I hear you're a hero, Gus!' said the judge as he flung open the door.

'Oh, sir! I'm that glad you are home!' Gustaf wrung out the mop, set it and the bucket of water near the stairway, and came back to report. But where did one begin such a tale? He looked at the judge anxiously and hunted in his mind for the right words.

'I saw the ruins.' The judge sat down in his great chair and lighted a long cigar. 'They say an Indian started the fire.'

'But he didn't, Judge Turner! Truly he didn't!' Suddenly, in a rush of words, part English, part Swedish, Gustaf told the whole story. Judge Turner listened patiently, rolling and twisting the cigar in his teeth, now and then blowing clouds of smoke to the ceiling. Gustaf told him everything, from the first glimpse of flame to the pony.

'You did fine, Gus,' approved the judge. 'We'll not say a word about Big Whistle. He has always had a fine reputation. A dozen men in town knew him when he was in the mission school. You'll learn, all too soon, that if anything happens and an Indian is in sight, he gets the blame. Indian trouble is brewing up north; we don't want to start any here.

'They tell me out there' — he pointed his cigar toward the street — 'that awhile ago they found bones in the ashes of the barn; human bones, someone said. Maybe Big Whistle was right in his surmise; Indians are smart that way. Say nothing of it and the town will soon forget. Already the Swiss is bargaining for lumber, and volunteers promise a barn-raising. People will help repair the stores, too. This will all blow over. . . I hear you have a new pony, Gus?' He laughed at Gustaf's anxious look.

190

'Yes, sir. And I'm that pleased. But where shall I keep him? And how'll I earn money for his feed?' Gustaf had been puzzling on these problems as he mopped the floors.

'How would you like to tend the cows for the Swiss? Milk morning and evening? He says he saw last spring you were a good milker. Soon he'll have his new barn; get him to give you room for your pony and some feed for pay. You might fetch straw and fodder from the prairie yourself.'

'I could make me a drag and bring prairie grass in to town. If you could spare me, sir.'

'That's a good idea. Yes, you can manage the time.' He chewed his cigar. Gustaf waited; he could see the judge had something on his mind.

'Fact of the matter is, Gus, several things have turned up. Lucius Hubbard was talking to me yesterday before I left. His new *Red Wing Republican* is a good little paper. But he needs more subscribers. He thinks he could get some out in the country.'

'Yes, sir.' As the judge paused, Gustaf looked at the pile of this new weekly newspaper; there had been seven issues. As soon as each was read, Gustaf folded it neatly and put it in the pile under the paperweight on the table.

'He thinks Swedes ought to subscribe.'

'The paper is printed in English. Few can read English, sir.'

'Norelius told him that. But children are going to school and learning fast. A Red Wing paper would keep country people in touch with markets and help the older ones learn English. No way better. If your people want to be good citizens, Gus, they have to know what's going on.'

'Yes, sir. That's just what my father said.'

'Hubbard wants you to try for a subscription in Vasa and one out your home way, for a start. Even two will help him make his paper known. He said he'd take the pay in produce. Maybe he would pay your commission in oats. Have to work deals out that way now when cash is so short.' Gustaf thought the idea over.

'Another thing,' continued the judge. 'That neighbor of yours, Edstrom, tried to buy windows and doors for a house. No more shipments will come up the river this fall. Yesterday I found that Potter hasn't money to build as he planned this fall. He'd like to sell the windows and doors that came on the last boat. But he will only sell for gold. Paper money's no good in this depression. Maybe you can get Potter and Edstrom together and make a good deal.'

'*I*, sir?'

'Who else? Potter talks English; Edstrom knows only Swedish. I hated to send you walking out there, near sixty miles for a couple of errands. Now you have a pony. Can you ride, Gus?'

'Oh, yes, sir! My grandfather Anders had a horse. I can ride. But can I do the business?'

'Of course. Carry a few copies of the paper; leave some in Vasa and one at each of the homesteads by your father's. I'll write a letter to Edstrom about the mill work. You read it to him in Swedish. He can send word back. It's a fine chance for him to get good material cheap. Potter will sell for less than cost if he can get gold.'

192

AN UNEXPECTED TRIP

'When should I go, sir?'

'Soon as we have dinner. I'm starved. You tidy yourself while I write the letter. After dinner I'll see Hubbard. You can get off in an hour.' Then he noticed the burned shirt. 'How's your burn, Son? Can you take a journey so soon?'

'Oh, yes, sir. Mrs. Albright fixed it. I'll be glad to get home for a shirt; this one is burned past my mending. Mother will put in a new sleeve, maybe.'

'Better ask Mrs. Albright to make sure it's all right to go. I declare I forgot about a saddle! I'll wager there isn't a saddle in town to fit that pony.'

'I rode Grandfather's horse bareback,' said Gustaf anxiously. Suppose the judge wouldn't let him go after all? He could hardly wait to show the pony to his family.

The judge frowned thoughtfully. Then his face brightened.

'I have it! The very thing! In my trunk over there is a heavy old blanket and a leather girth. If you rode bareback, you can ride with a blanket strapped on. The pony will like it better than a saddle. Open that trunk in the corner; it's not locked.'

Gustaf opened the great Saratoga trunk and lifted out the covered tray. In the lower part was a jumble of clothes, books, and papers; the blanket was at the bottom. He found no strap.

'I remember. It's in the tray just where my sister put it when she packed. There.'

Gustaf took out a great roll of leather and shut the trunk.

'Now I'll get at my letter while you straighten. Then

193

we'll have dinner and give the pony a tryout. They say he's broken but I want to see how he acts before you go.'

'I don't look very nice to eat dinner with you, Judge,' Gustaf said shyly. 'My shirt's so torn and I haven't cleaned my coat yet.'

'What's the difference?' growled the judge. 'Think I'm going to miss the chance of walking up Main Street with the hero just for a burned shirt? Run along while I write that letter.' For a second time the judge used that word, 'hero.' Gustaf didn't know the meaning. He must look it up in 'Webster's Speller' as soon as he had a chance.

The judge opened his inkwell, picked up his long pen, and started writing. Gustaf carried the scrub bucket and mop downstairs, emptied the dirty water into the gutter by the plank sidewalk, shook out the mop, and hung both bucket and mop by the back door. Then he washed at the pump and smoothed his hair before the mirror hung by the door.

'Have you named your pony?' asked the judge as they finished dinner.

'I've been thinking of names, sir, but I can't seem to make it real that he's mine.'

'Take a ride on him and you'll feel different,' advised the judge. They walked over to the stable yard where Ranger and the pony were now tied. 'Put the blanket on him and canter down the street. I'll see how you manage. If it's all right, we'll get the papers and you can start off at once.'

Gustaf folded the blanket across the pony's back and fastened the strap. The pony looked around, interested.

AN UNEXPECTED TRIP

As soon as Gustaf mounted, the pony was off down the street. At the corner of Plum Street, they passed Nels, who stopped to stare at the disappearing pony and rider. Around three blocks the pony dashed, then Gustaf turned him home.

Judge Turner was a bit anxious. Could Gustaf hold the pony? He went out into the street; looked up and down. No boy on a pony was in sight. A couple of minutes later they came around the corner by Weatherby's store, the pony under good control, Gustaf grinning.

'Well, he went like greased lightning, I'd say,' laughed the judge, relieved.

'"Lightning!" That's the right name for him, sir. I'm naming him "Lightning."'

'Fine, Gus. You'd better watch him or you'll be home before you start. Now we'll go to the newspaper office. I reckon you'd rather go home first and stop by Vasa coming back.'

Gustaf flushed. The judge seemed to know everything.

'You see, sir, I never expected to have a pony, never.'

'I'd like to be there when you get to your home. Won't their eyes pop? If I didn't have this claim on my hands I'd go along just to see. I declare I would.'

Chapter Twenty-Five

'WHO's there?' Larsson's voice called sharply into the darkness.

'It's Gus, Father.'

'*Gus!*' The father was astonished. 'What's happened?'

'Oh, everything! Everything! Just wait till you hear; you'll hardly believe. I want to surprise them, Father!' Gustaf slid off the pony and, holding the bridle tightly, walked to meet his father near the sod house. Silver sheen from a quarter-moon spread over the prairie, making light enough for them to see the pony.

'Mother! Elna! Hans! Ernst!' the boy shouted.

196

NEW EXPERIENCES

'Come!' All afternoon he had planned this moment. Now he was so excited he could hardly speak.

They rushed from the house, Hans and Elna rubbing their eyes; they had been sound asleep. Ernst was not there; the others stared at Gustaf and the pony.

'He's mine, Mother! The pony's mine. A present because I saved the horses.'

'I'll tend the pony, Son,' the father spoke quietly. 'You'd better go in and rest. You've come too fast. The excitement has clean gone to your head.'

Gustaf laughed.

'I'll tend him myself, Father,' he answered, calmer now. 'He just needs a little water and oats, now, till he gets rested. I remember how Grandfather Anders used to treat a horse. If you'll hold the bridle, I'll be back in a minute.' He tossed the bridle to his father, ran for a measure of oats, brought a pailful of water from the creek, and then tied Lightning to a sapling near-by. 'Now, then, I'll tell you.' His family had waited, speechless, while he hurried about; now they followed him into the sod house.

'You want some supper, Gus.' The mother found her voice first. She stirred the fire and pulled the coffee-pot to the front on the stove. 'I've some fish; I'll make hot corn cakes for you.'

'Anything will do, Mother. Anything you cook is good.' Gustaf drank a dipperful of water from the pail standing in the corner and sat down. 'Now I'll tell you.'

As they listened to the tale Gustaf had for them, the mother warmed the fish and fried corn cakes on a new iron griddle she had acquired only last week from passing settlers who traded it for potatoes. She had wanted to

197

show Gustaf the griddle; now she didn't think to speak of it, she was so busy listening to his story. The cakes all but burned when she forgot to turn them. Such happenings to her own boy! Elna and Hans listened, round-eyed; Larsson pulled at a lock of blond hair exactly as Gustaf often did when he was excited. They couldn't believe it all. Yet the pony was there, real.

They talked until midnight. Suddenly the mother remembered that Gustaf had slept but little in the old mission cabin, the night before.

'Selfish creatures that we are!' she exclaimed, 'keeping you from your rest, Gus. I'll change the bandage on your shoulder; luckily I have some fresh unsalted butter handy. You shall have a shirt of your father's to take back with you and I'll make you a new one of your own, maybe two, before Christmas. The new flax is fine; I'm already at the spinning. Yours shall be made the first. Now you children are not to ask another question. Gus must get his rest.' Meekly, Hans lay down on the trundle bed; Elna rolled into her narrow cot and Gustaf climbed onto the bunk above. He *was* sleepy, for a fact.

He took the letter to Mr. Edstrom in the morning and wrote the answer in which Edstrom agreed to take the mill work and left the terms for Judge Turner to arrange. An hour later, Vanberg came over to the Larsson place on an errand and the whole wonderful tale must be told for the third time. This Sunday there was no service in Vasa; the men had time to listen. Edstrom and Vanberg both subscribed to the *Red Wing Republican*.

Lightning seemed fine after his long journey; Indian ponies were used to crossing the prairies. Gustaf started for Vasa before noon.

NEW EXPERIENCES

'I'd like to stay, Mother,' Gustaf replied to her urging, 'but I mustn't miss school. And I told Nels I'd be back for the milking tomorrow morning.' Hans and Elna each had a ride on Lightning; the mother put good food in Gustaf's pocket and exclaimed at the way his father's shirt set on Gustaf's widening shoulders.

'Be sure you come home for Christmas, Son,' she called. 'You grow so fast we won't know you if you stay longer.'

'I'll be here, Mother; the judge promised me. You may count on it.' He rode away, leaving them staring. Even now the whole thing seemed like a dream.

The trip was a success and Judge Turner was very pleased. Gustaf had sold the building material and got five subscribers for the newspaper. Delivery wouldn't be much of a worry as long as the pastor's school was in session, for someone went out Vasa way nearly every week, and would willingly carry the papers. School children would take them on home from there. Later, neighbors would take turns fetching the papers from Vasa. The judge sent the building material out on two carts; now that harvest was over men were glad to do hauling. They hoped to stay and help with the building and earn a little extra.

'You're quite a business man, Gus,' the judge approved when the boy gave his report late that Sunday evening. They ate crackers and milk together and talked over the trip. 'I told you we need someone for a go-between for the Swedes and the rest of us. You'll work up a good business before you open a law book if you don't watch out. The law will be a help to you though, even now. You ought to be learning how to make a contract. I'll

199

plan out some reading for you so you can get started.'
He crumbled more crackers into his bowl. 'But you've
done enough for this week. Lightning needs a rest and
so do you. Take it easy for a few days, Son. That boy
Nels, you like him?'

'Oh yes, sir! But I don't see him often. We go to different schools, you know.'

'By spring he will go to the town school, your pastor
says. You hunt him up this week, Gus, and play around
a bit. Do you good.' Gustaf looked at him puzzled. He
had never heard advice like that. The judge pushed his
empty bowl aside and reached for a book. Gustaf
washed the bowls, set them in the cupboard, and got out
his Bible. This hadn't seemed like Sunday. He read
two chapters and then went to bed. Already the burned
shoulder was more comfortable; soon it would be well.

Four days later he saw Nels. 'Hello, Gus,' Nels called
cheerfully as he hurried up the street.

'Wait a minute, Nels. I've been looking for you.'

'Come along, then,' answered Nels. 'I have a new job.
Have to hurry.'

'A job? Out this way?' Gustaf was surprised. He
didn't know of any business out in this direction; the
stores were south of here. North, there were only a
few sheds, small cabins, and the great clay bank. He
caught up with Nels and they walked on briskly.

'Yes, a fine job, Gus. I've wanted to see you to tell
you. I got it the day before the fire; then you went away.
My job's at the stoneware works.'

Gustaf stared. The stoneware works? Then he remembered.

'You mean out by the clay pit?'

NEW EXPERIENCES

Nels nodded.

'There's a new man came to Red Wing this fall from St. Louis, Chris Graham. He can't do much this fall because cold weather will stop him unless he gets a good building built. But he has an oven and he's fired some pieces already. He says this clay makes a beautiful color of stoneware. So far, he makes things on a foot-turned wheel he brought with him, but come spring he plans to build a water wheel and do a big business. I'm helping.'

Gustaf shoved back his hair and looked again at Nels. The lad seemed gay and happy. His eyes sparkled as he talked.

'You like it?' he said.

'Oh, yes, Gus! A potter makes things with his hands. It's much better than studying. I want to stop school, come spring, and work here all the time.' Gustaf found that hard to understand. 'You can do studying for the two of us,' laughed Nels. 'Here we are!'

They entered a small shed open on one side, facing the clay bank. A man sat by the potter's wheel treading briskly, shaping a large butter crock as the wheel spun around. He grinned at them but didn't slow up his work.

'Showing off the place to a friend of yours, Nels?' he asked. 'He won't think much of it now. But you wait, Son. Some day this is going to be the biggest business in Red Wing. Known the country over.'

'We must hire Gus for our lawyer, Mr. Graham,' said Nels. 'Gus is going to be a great lawyer some day.' He grinned at Gustaf. 'I'll be a partner in the stoneware works.'

'Then we've got that settled. Takes a boy to fix up the future.' He stopped the wheel and inspected his work. 'If you ask me, I think it would do more good to let the future alone and fetch me some wood. I'm nearly ready to fire. Want to try your hand at making something, Gus?' Mr. Graham had a round, friendly face and wide side whiskers. He smiled at Gustaf kindly.

'I wouldn't know what to make, sir. I never tried, you see.'

'Isn't there anything you want, Gus?' prompted Nels. He was pleased with the kindness Mr. Graham showed to Gustaf. 'You know, Mr. Graham, Gus is the boy who saved the horses. He lives with Judge Turner.' The potter nodded.

'I'd be right pleased to have you try your hand,' he said again. 'You may think you want to be a lawyer, but you can't be sure till you've tried a potter's wheel. Most interesting work in the world. Eh, Nels?'

Gustaf stood silent, puzzled. Then a thought came to him.

'Could I make a flowerpot, sir?'

'A flowerpot?' Graham was amazed. 'Never thought of such a thing. How big? What would you do with it?' He rubbed his chin thoughtfully and looked at Gustaf.

'You'd grow a plant in it. Make it about so' — he measured some four or five inches high and four inches in diameter. 'Ladies like them for keeping plants by the window. My mother does, I know. Could I make one, do you think?'

'Of course. You've given me an idea, too.' He jumped up, grabbed a hunk of clay from the bucket in the corner. 'What color do you want it, Son?'

202

NEW EXPERIENCES

'Color? Can you make different colors?'

'Sure as anything. My secret method. I mix the color in the clay now. Some day I'll have a glaze that will beat anything you've ever seen.'

'I'd like red,' Gustaf decided, and watched the potter mold the clay and slap it onto his wheel.

'Sit here and turn it yourself. Nels; get that kiln to warming so we can bake this. Gus isn't going to vanish. He'll be working at this same clay ten minutes from now.'

Awkwardly, Gustaf worked the pedal up and down, up and down until he got the rhythm.

'Now, then, put your thumbs in the center so, and push down gently. Keep that treadle going! *Keep her going!* This may not take as much brains as law but it takes *some!*' Good-humoredly coaxing and scolding he kept Gustaf at it until his fingers shaped a fairly round pot something like the size and shape he had in mind.

'Not bad! Not bad,' said the potter. 'I'll finish it off for you now.' Gustaf gave his place at the wheel to the potter, and with a few turns of the wheel the rough bowl became smooth and round. The potter stopped to inspect it.

'I believe you've got something there, Gus,' he said finally. Nels had the fire under the kiln going briskly now and stepped over to look, too. 'They tell me in town that no one will buy my things; on account of the depression you know, boys. But if I can think up *small* things people really want, I'll get going fine.' He looked pleased and happy.

'Come around in a day or two, Gus. I'll fire this for you and you can carry it to your mother next time you go home.'

203

'That will not be till Christmas, sir.'

'No matter. It will make her a fine Christmas present. You'll be pleased when it's fired, Gus. It'll come out rosy red. She'll like to show it to her friends. Tell her it's Red Wing Stoneware. Doesn't that have a stylish sound, boys?'

Gustaf stayed around until milking time, helping Nels keep the kiln at even temperature, gathering wood for the next day. Maybe the judge wouldn't call this loafing but it surely was fun. And think how pleased his mother would be with her gift.

ANOTHER CHRISTMAS

Chapter Twenty-Six

DECEMBER snow whitened the prairie, protected the winter wheat. Gustaf shaded his eyes and looked toward the western glow. The sun had set half an hour ago; the wind blew colder every minute. Lightning would be glad for shelter; Gustaf was hungry as the pony. Yesterday's storm passed over, luckily; the men in Red Wing predicted that he could make the journey out and back before the January blizzards. Over the next rise, he spied smoke from the sod house chimney and the gleam of a candle set in the window.

Days since his hurried visit in November had been so busy he could hardly realize that five weeks had gone by. Milking, morning and evening, for the hotelkeeper, and the care of Lightning took every spare moment. Evenings, Judge Turner often had him copy papers. The judge liked Gustaf's handwriting and said that copying legal notes was the best way to learn law. The pony was a great bit of good fortune, for on Lightning Gustaf did errands for the judge or for Mr. Hubbard.

Now he tied the bridle around a sapling and went toward the sod house.

'Mother! Gus is here!' Elna tossed aside her knitting as the door opened.

'I'm glad, Son. It's getting cold out.' The mother had worried about the storm. 'Supper is ready to dish up. We hoped you'd come today. Ernst said not to wait for him. Did Edstrom give you my letter? And the list?'

'Aye, Mother. I mailed the letter at once. Edstrom left the wheat with the miller and I have part of the flour hung over Lightning's back. Here are the other things.' He carefully lifted a bundle from his shoulder and laid it on the bed. 'Don't touch that till I come,' he warned Elna. 'I'll tend Lightning; it won't take long.' When he came back, he washed his hands, warmed them by the stove, and they sat down to supper.

'The miller says your wheat is good, Father; but you'll get better next year from Weatherby's seed. They talk of building a mill in Vasa, come spring. Red Wing's a long way to carry wheat for grinding.

'I got your wool, Mother, it's clean and smooth; you'll like it. I brought you some blue calico, too; it came up the river on the last boat of the season. Mr. Hubbard sent you two papers, Father. He likes the idea I suggested. He has one column in Swedish in each paper with news of markets and Swedish families. The Swiss asked about you, Mother; says he never forgets your cooking Elna, he sent candy to you and Hans for a Christmas treat.'

ANOTHER CHRISTMAS

'Oh, Gus, *really?*' Elna was thrilled.

'May we eat some now?' asked Hans as Gustaf pulled the small sack from his pocket.

'Didn't you hear Gus say it's Christmas candy, Son?' The mother put the sack on the shelf. 'Come Christmas Eve, you'll be glad you saved it.'

'He sent you store bread from the new bakery, Mother. But yours is much better.'

She smiled at him as she ladled bowlfuls of steaming porridge and spooned over each a rich gravy with hunks of meat, delicious stewed muskrat, tasty and hot. Supper was a feast in honor of Gustaf's return, with rye cakes, jam, and cheese for a finish.

'*Now* you'll open the bundle,' Elna said. Curiosity had nearly spoiled her supper.

Gustaf looked around the tiny room. Where could he keep a surprise for four whole days? It would be better to give his mother her gift now than to risk breaking it. The geranium slip was growing nicely, he'd noticed. The father had sawed a short length of a small sapling and hollowed a hole for the dirt. 'I'll have to tease Elna a bit,' Gustaf thought to himself, 'and I'll not give her *her* present till Christmas Eve.' He had carved a tiny locket from a peach stone the hotelkeeper had given him. Now he glanced at the bundle on the bed.

'Oh, those are Mother's things; wool and calico and the newspapers.'

'And something else,' insisted Elna. Gustaf grinned at her and opened the bundle.

Folded in with the hanks of wool was the flowerpot. He unwound the wool slowly, enjoying their suspense, and held the rosy red jar before them.

207

'Your Christmas present, Mother. I made it for you at the new stoneware works in town. It's for your geranium.'

'*My* present?' she was astonished. Gustaf handed it to her and she turned it round and round for them all to see. Fingermarks as the wheel turned had traced a pattern on the outside; candlelight reflected from the rosy glaze. It was a pretty thing.

'Mrs. Albright says to put a few tiny stones and dry leaves in the bottom; then plant the geranium and set it at the window.' The mother could not find words, she was so pleased. Gustaf understood her silence.

'You're so grown up, Son,' she said at last. 'I'm proud. I thank you.'

At that minute Ernst burst into the room. Candles flickered with the flurry of cold wind as the door was flung open. Ernst had been working some four miles north and had run most of the way home in his eagerness to see Gustaf. While he ate his supper they told him Gustaf's news and the mother allowed him to hold the flowerpot.

After supper he eyed Gustaf thoughtfully.

'You look pretty knowing, Gus. Maybe you haven't told everything yet.'

'You're knowing, yourself, to guess,' laughed Gustaf. 'Maybe I have a job for you.'

'A job for me?' Ernst hadn't expected that.

'Oh, Gus! Where?' asked Elna.

'Moving a steamboat to Red River.' Gustaf spoke casually and laughed at their amazed stares. He had planned to surprise them.

'Where's Red River?' Ernst asked.

'A big steamboat?' inquired Elna.

'Who's moving it?' Larsson wanted to know.

'Would Ernst be a sailor?' Hans liked that idea.

'Let Gus tell us,' commanded the father. 'Begin at the beginning, Son.'

'Red River is a couple of hundred miles or more west. The people out there have offered a bonus of a thousand dollars to the man who puts a boat on that river. A thousand dollars is a lot of money any time, but this winter city men are so poor that many talk of trying for the money. Anson Northup has a boat, the *North Star*, on the upper Mississippi for carrying lumbermen's supplies; it's laid up at Crow Wing River now.'

The children leaned on the table, fascinated, the candy quite forgotten.

'Now Northup plans to take his boat apart and load it on wagons. He says he'll saw it up if need be. Thirty to forty teams will haul the whole thing — engines, cabins, hull, and furniture. A. R. Young, one of his men, is in Red Wing now engaging help for the trip. They'll pay two dollars a day and board from the time a man gets to Crow Wing. Start in February and hope to be across the territory to LaFayette before thaw. The men must agree to stay and assemble the boat out there.' Gustaf studied Ernst's face.

'Straight west, you say?' the father asked.

'Yes. There are no roads, no one knows the country. But they'll get there.'

'Are *you* going, Gus?' the mother asked suddenly.

'Oh, no! I'd rather stay with Judge Turner. He counts on me. But it will be a fine adventure. I told Young about you, Ernst. You'd have to be in Red Wing

the last of January. Pastor Norelius will bring word
when he comes if you can't decide now. It's a good
chance to see the country and earn at the same time.'

They were all silent, thinking.

'The pastor will be in Vasa for Christmas,' the mother
remarked. '*Julotta* is at five o'clock.'

'Some talk of building a church near here next summer,' Gustaf remembered. 'More families are coming
west this spring. Pastor Norelius would get it started.
People like him.'

'The township is getting settled fast,' the mother added.
She turned to her spinning wheel, fingering the new wool.
Elna and Hans cleared up the supper. The father,
Ernst, and Gustaf went out to tend the stock. Ernst's
chance needed thought, not talk.

'It's lucky Ernst doesn't have to go right now,' the
mother remarked after the men came back. 'Carl will
need his help cutting logs for our new house.'

'Oh, we may let that job go till another year.' Larsson
spoke easily, rubbing his chilled hands by the stove.
'It's not important.'

'Not important?' cried the mother. 'Should we live in
this sod house another *year?* Are we gophers to spend our
lives in a hole in the ground?' Anna Marie's eyes flashed.
By her wheel, she stood with arms akimbo, staring at her
husband.

'Water dripping through the roof with every rain!
Dripping on beds, on food. Leaking at every little thaw.
A sod house is no proper home for a Larsson.'

The father studied her silently. No word was spoken
in the tiny room. The others looked at the mother with
awe; they had never heard her speak so. Always she

agreed that whatever the father did was right. This surely was a remarkable evening.

Quietly Larsson looked around the room as though he saw it for the first time. In the candlelight he saw spots of stain on the ceiling cloth; dirt dropped from walls lay in heaps along the edges; the room was never clean. He recalled, now, that water dripped onto beds, food, and the loom. The sod house was not as good shelter as the Pine Lake cabin, though warmer. It looked dreary; the gay shawl could not hang against dirt walls.

'You are right, Wife, to speak up for your home. Boys, we'll start felling logs tomorrow. We'll use you while you're here, Gus. With luck we'll have enough down time Ernst goes.' (Ernst's going seemed accepted.) 'I and the ox will haul the logs over by spring. I suppose you have the house all planned,' he teased his wife.

'That I have!' she replied, laughing. 'I plan while I spin. A large room for our living with a small room to the west for my parents and Greta when they come over. A lean-to at the back for a workroom; a loft for the boys. You'll be back for the summer, Gus, surely.'

As she turned toward Gustaf, she noticed a happy far-away look on Ernst's face. 'Greta will be glad when they come, too,' she said kindly. 'And some day, Ernst, you may have your own house on the south forty. Carl will help you build when the time comes. You will help him this spring. We'll have a nice home.' She smiled affectionately at her husband and started her wheel whirling. The father was a good man; interested in his family, not just in money-making as some men were.

'Maybe they'll get the letter I mailed in time to come out this summer,' said Gustaf. 'Trains run to New York every week even in winter, it's said. Mail is fast, now.'

On the morning of the twenty-fourth, Gustaf went with Ernst to release his traps; one wouldn't, of course, capture any creature on Christmas Eve. At noon, Hans tied a great, beautiful sheaf of wheat atop a post east of the house. Birds arrived by the score. Hans called the family to admire the wheat, the best of the harvest, set aside for this occasion.

The Christmas tree was green and beautiful and the children trimmed it at twilight. The mother had baked star cookies decorated with red store sugar Gustaf brought. These made handsome ornaments along with orange and red berries, yarn and candles. With plenty of butter and flour, the Christmas baking was fine this year; Ernst was a good trapper, the meat pies were large and luscious. With Ernst and Gustaf away, the father had had no time to make toys this year. But Elna and Hans were happy with friends and school; toys were not needed.

Christmas psalms, supper, and candle-lighting ceremonies were early and all went to bed. The start for Vasa was set for three o'clock.

Elna was so excited she could hardly sleep. Her new hood, with red-and-blue embroidery, she had made herself, was very becoming. The peach-stone locket hung from a length of blue yarn. Wooden shoes were stained with walnut juice as Breta had taught her; they looked almost the color of leather. Some day, her father promised, when the land was paid for, she should have a pair of store shoes.

Gustaf, rolled in his blanket on the floor, wakened in

the night; his thoughts turned to Red Wing. Judge Turner had gone to St. Paul over the holidays, Nels was doing the milking. In two days Gustaf meant to start back. He heard his mother get up and spoke to her.

'Oh, are you awake, Gus?' she whispered. 'I'm going to look at the stars.' She crept to the window, lifted the curtain, and looked out. 'Must be two hours after midnight. Don't wake the others. I'll get the fire going and make the coffee. Then we'll call them.'

Gustaf folded his blanket neatly. 'I'll tend the stock for father,' he whispered. 'We'd better start early. Maybe we'll meet the Edstroms on the way.' Soon the sod house glowed with light.

Laughing and joking, the Larssons got themselves dressed, ate breakfast, and did the chores. Many families would come to Vasa by oxcart or hand-pulled sled, bringing babies or older folk. The Larssons were all able and vigorous, they would walk; it was warmer, really. The mother came from the sod house last; she had banked the fire, Gustaf had piled wood handy, ready to start it up quickly on the return. They walked briskly.

Across the prairie they heard music. Elna and Gustaf paused to listen. It was 'Dolph's oboe, playing the Swedish Christmas hymn.

> All hail to thee, O blessèd morn.
> To tidings long by prophets borne
> Hast thou fulfillment given.
>
> O sacred and immortal day
> When unto earth in glorious ray
> Descends the grace of heaven!

213

THEY CAME FROM SWEDEN

Singing,
Ringing,
Sounds are blending,
Praises sending
Unto heaven
For the Saviour to us given.

Johan Olof Wallin, 1814.

'They're on ahead!' cried Elna, 'and we're not halfway there yet. We can catch them.' She turned to Gustaf. "Dolph has taught us the Christmas hymn, Gus. We can sing it in four parts, now. It's beautiful. He comes over to Vasa once a week to teach us music. He's going to play in the service this morning.'

'When I come home for spring planting, I'm going to ask him to teach me,' said Gustaf. 'There's a new family coming out in the spring; the father plays the fiddle. We ought to have nice music this summer.'

'Think of that!' exclaimed the mother. 'Seems as though we have *everything*.'

'Hello! Wait for us!' the Vanbergs shouted from a southerly direction. The Edstroms heard, too, and both families waited for the others to catch up. This meeting of friends on the way to *Julotta* was like old times. Ahead, in the village, candlelight was gleaming in every window, glowing on the snow in welcome. Here on the prairie the children sang as they waited in the crisp starlight.

'It's like the Holy Night,' Mrs. Larsson whispered to her husband. 'Singing and stars.'

In a pause between songs, Elna turned to her brother.

'Let's hang on the Edstroms' runners, Gus. It's fun, isn't it?'

'Aye,' he agreed. 'I like it. I'm glad we came to America.'